Walking in the Shadow

Stories of Life, Death,
and the Southern Funeral Home

Walking in the Shadow

Stories of Life, Death, and the Southern Funeral Home

D.S. Bradley

Muddy Ford Press

Chapin, South Carolina

Walking in the Shadow: Stories of Life, Death, and the Southern Funeral Home. Copyright 2016 by D.S. Bradley. All rights reserved. Printed in the United States of America. No part of this book may be used or reproduced in any manner whatsoever without written permission from the author except in the case of brief quotations embodied in critical reviews and articles. Contact Muddy Ford Press, 1009 Muddy Ford Road, Chapin, SC 29036

Library of Congress Number: 2016917488

ISBN: 978-1-942081-08-1

Note: The names of the characters in Walking in the Shadow *have all been changed to protect both the living and the dead.*

cover photo by Sadie Bradley

Contents

Preface

My parents came from working class roots, backgrounds
fuzzy with cotton-mill lint and seasoned with sweat. They had
not gone to college via the traditional route, and in keeping with many Baby Boomers, they retained much of their
parents' mistrust of liberal education. Like most parents, they
wanted "a better life" for their children. Like most children,
I didn't understand their apprehension about the prospect
of four years' worth of student loans, a "useless" English
degree, and a longing to … write.

Eight months beyond graduation, after hanging onto a fun
college job with no real future while I worked on an ambi-
tious first novel, my new bride gently reminded me that the
time had come to find a "real" job. A failed attempt at running a vending machine route left me physically tired and
mentally stunted. I knew by my second week of slapping
crackers and candy bars into machines all over the metro
Greenville, South Carolina, area from 4:30 in the morning
until sometimes 6:00 in the evening that a job like that would
eventually drive me to run that silver and black snack truck
into the murky waters of Lake Hartwell, turn my back, and
walk away from a widening slick of canned soda and cello-
phane-wrapped chicken-sandwich flotsam.

To the day I called the local funeral home, the number for
which I picked out of the phone book, my exposure to that
other side of life had been confined to little more than one
dead great-grandmother and a high-school classmate killed in
a car wreck. My parents? They just shook their heads at the
idea of funeral home work.

That first day on the job was like walking into another world where the vast secrets of a part of life recognized but ignored came spilling out around every corner. The bowels of the funeral home, a dark, oil-smelling garage bay on one side and a bright, sugary-chemical scented embalming room, dressing room, and casket selection room on the other side captivated me. Deep wooden racks held plastic-draped caskets (I ignorantly called them coffins on that first day) crafted out of oak, poplar, pecan, mahogany, and, yes, pine. The oft reminisced "pine box," I soon learned, is neither cheap nor roughly knocked together in the fashion alluded to by country songs and Southern writers.

Mack, the man who showed me around that day, would become my mentor as I began my funeral education. I asked him what was inside the giant metal safe whose outside was devoid of its original burnish after many years of sitting in a basement that felt the effects of seasonal changes more than the rest of the building.

"Cremains," he said.

"Cre-what?"

"Cremated human remains."

Dr. Margaret Wooten, my undergraduate mentor and English professor, one of the people who believed in me when my writing was still pretty unbelievable (and not in a good way) would have called the people who work in the funeral business "characters." Mack was certainly one. Like the dearly departed we ushered to their places of final repose, the living human beings, wraithlike in their own ways, who inhabited the funeral home came in all shapes, sizes, and religious affiliations. Some of the men were happily married to their high-school sweethearts; some of the men were just married, no adverbs necessary. Some had no affiliation whatsoever. Most of them went to church on their Sundays off; a few actually believed what they heard preached. There were some drinkers, more than a few heavy smokers. One man golfed to relieve the stress; another worked on old cars.

The people, families and employees alike, I've had the pleasure and displeasure to work with through the years, have provided me with a lifetime of subtle lessons and tacit directives: Life is indeed short. People lose their minds when stricken with grief. Death cruelly, abruptly terminates all lines of communication between the deceased and estranged family members. Visitations can become parties. Be careful what you say; sometimes it's not a "good evening." Dark suit + long-sleeve shirt + parking cars for two hours when it's 98 degrees = misery. Don't refer to the dead person using the pronoun *it*. Not even Tide will get blood stains out of a white dress shirt. Embalming usually makes the person appear younger. Regret comes too late. We are definitely what we eat. Love your family while they're still with you, but do it like you know you're one day going to lose them.

"Funeral directors don't retire," Mack told me that evening during my first visitation. "They usually die working."

"What about the man I replaced?" I asked.

"Lung cancer."

"And the guy you told me about who used to work on the other shift?"

"Heart attack."

Most of the families I've met were just like my own family: proud, small-town mothers and fathers, grandmas and grandpas who sought the strength to get through yet another trial. They worked all week in the mill or at the shop, paid their bills, and sat on a pew every Sunday. Death, the final certainty that will one day greet us all, crept out of the life's shadows and cut down their beloveds without a second thought.

Spending more than twenty years working in a funeral home
has certainly provided enough stories for this writer, and the
stories in this collection are the result of an active imagination
during long hours parking cars or lingering at the cemetery as
well as an amalgamation of my own experiences or the color-
ful stories that frequent this way of life. Eddie, Jack, George,
Carl, Tim, Holman, Greg, and Mack guided me through the
early years when I undertook a life, well, undertaking. Despite
my parents' initial misgivings, my life in the shadow turned
out to be anything but ordinary.

A Better Place

We weren't just poor; we were ignorant, and ignorance beats poverty by a mile. When teenagers who'd lived their short lives in a town that served as the butt of jokes finally had the chance to escape their predetermined fate after high school graduation, many willingly chose to stay. Said they wanted to work in the cotton mill – lint heads people called 'em – beside their daddies and granddaddies. What powerful force could keep so-called "educated" people from escaping, from admitting to a soft, inbred lethargy that gnawed away at the town's collective soul? Ignorance. Only ignorance could stifle the universal, bone-deep need to stretch our wings and fly on our own.

That was the reason I chose to leave: an escape from the dreadful ignorance. I would travel to a not-so-faraway city in the fall to, according to my grandma, "get some learnin'." But the town's elder schoolchildren still had other formalities to attend to before a few of us could attempt flight; graduation came on a hot June evening, the first Friday of the month. Fifty-seven of us would walk across Mr. Cann's flatbed trailer parked on the rutted football field; forty-two of us would actually get diplomas.

"Dang, it's hot under this robe," my friend Chris said.

"It's called a gown," Ida corrected. "Now, you losers stay put. I'm expected up at the front of the line."

She gave us a quick wink before throwing an obvious scowl toward the bleachers. Her daddy was up there, an ornery man whose temperament was made somewhat bearable by a woman, Ida's mother, whose pleasantness set all situations at ease. Ida was glad to finally be rid of him.

Valedictorians traditionally lead the procession during the graduation ceremony, and Ida Bone had worked too hard and sacrificed for too long to let anything or anybody stand in the way of what was rightfully hers. She had a plan.

"There's no way I'm staying in this hole and working in that mill like my mama and daddy," she often reminded us. "I'm going to college and make some opportunity for myself."

And we all knew she would. Chris and I had both been accepted to the colleges of our choice and would go on to concentrate in business and English respectively, but Ida's plan did not include such pedestrian pursuits. No, she had been accepted to Clemson University, and her goal was to major in biology and then head off to medical school in Charleston. "I'm gonna be a cardiologist," she proclaimed. And none of us doubted for a second that she would make it all happen.

When my mother told me over breakfast on Sunday morning that Miss Nell from across the street had called to tell her about a bad wreck the night before, I shrugged, drank the rest of my milk, and headed to the bathroom to finish getting ready for church. Miss Nell didn't have any details.

I met Chris on the stairs leading up to the second floor of Pineview Baptist Church, and we took the steps two and a time to avoid being late again for Sunday school.

"I know this is a shock," we heard our teacher Mrs. Temple say as we burst through the door. Instead of a rowdy, talking-at-the-same-time group of a dozen or so teenagers sitting in the metal chairs that lined the scuffed and scraped walls, we were met by red eyes and sagging heads. We stood there for a moment taking in the scene, and then I saw the empty chair – Ida.

"She and her little brother Craig were killed," Mrs. Temple continued. "They were on their way home from their grandparents' house." She sniffled. "Her mother said it was a family graduation celebration."

That was the first time I remember being so close to death's fickleness. I was barely eighteen years old myself, and God wasn't supposed to allow young people to die, at least not in our little town. Old people got sick, suffered for a few years, and ultimately succumbed to their varied ailments. But eighteen year old girls on their way to greatness were supposed to live.

I'm not sure what Mrs. Temple's lesson was about that morning – the Sermon on the Mount, I think – for my thoughts lay fixed on Ida. We'd been friends for as long as any of us had been alive. Nine of us shared March birthdays, and Ida and I were born in the same hospital one day apart.

Chris and I joined some more of our friends two nights later in the parking lot of the little funeral home on Main Street. I was the last to cross the threshold into a realm where I had yet to find myself thus far in my young life. My great-grandmother had died when I was boy, but what's the death of an eighty-four year old woman who lived nearly four hours away to a six year old?

Old fashioned gas lamps long-converted to run on electricity lined the narrow hallway, and at the end of the hall, a broad staircase disappeared into the second-floor shadows.

"You all must be here to view young Ida Bone," the tall man said.

I looked up with a start to see Mr. Pursely, the funeral home's gaunt owner, pointing a long, bent finger toward the brightly lit room to our right.

"Y'all go on in."

The white casket with pink shading seemed to blend into the wallpaper, and at the head end Ida's parents stood ready to greet the next person in line. Craig Bone, an eight-year-old who was small for his age, lay in quiet repose in another casket on the other side of the withered parents. My friends trudged past Ida's body with the lumbering gait and averted eyes of prisoners off to hard labor. None of us wanted to be there, yet each of us felt the deep kinship and conferred responsibility of showing what my grandfather called "respects." I honestly didn't know what that meant, but I knew I had to be there.

The wreck had undoubtedly broken Ida's body in ways my mind could hardly conceive, bends and breaks and tears that human flesh and bone were not meant to endure. Upon a girl who hardly wore any make up at all, Mr. Pursely had slathered a ghastly layer of beige face paint. One eye, her left, was just a bit higher than the other, and the darkened skin beneath it bulged. Ida's smile, the one that quieted many a teacher or bully throughout the years, broke through the wax and lipstick, and if her chin hadn't been awkwardly cocked to the right, that smile would have been perfect.

"Her jaw was broken in several places," Mr. Pursely whispered into my ear. "But she's in a better place."

Over the years I've found myself wondering if grieving families really take comfort in the often whispered, "Better place." The term has become a comic platitude, especially for those people who don't actually believe the deceased has gone on to some better place. But Mr. Pursely was right: Ida was in a better place, a place free of her manic daddy and her depressed mamma. A place free from the stresses of life.

Escape was the word the preacher used at the service the next day. "Escape from life's sorrows," he said. "Escape from the ignorance, meanness, and selfishness of this world."

When the soloist sang, "A better world awaitin'," I knew that Ida had found that world. She'd found an escape from life's human and necessary desires, escape from the ignorance she so sought to conquer.

So, when I graduated from college and still didn't have any real idea about how I wanted to spend my life, I one day turned to the funeral home, and I couldn't help thinking of Ida Bone. I remembered how broken her body looked in that casket, and I realized that for all the reasons I wanted to experience a life so foreign to me, understanding how I might have fixed up my friend so that the memory all of us had of her would have been a little more pleasant was on my mind. No, I didn't turn out to be even slightly proficient at the restorative arts, but I've worked with several embalmers through the years who would have skillfully turned young Ida Bone back into a picture of the future cardiologist we knew as our friend.

The Bone

A long-entrenched hierarchy exists in the Southern funeral home. From the top down, it goes something like this: owner, licensed funeral director, secretary, funeral assistants (men and women without funeral director's licenses), custodian, and the guy who cuts the grass and washes the cars.

From the perspective of just about everybody who works in the funeral home, the secretaries have it made because they have little offices that protect them from rainy days, blistering summer sun, and cemeteries where the wind and cold boarder on arctic. Their lunch breaks come at the same time every day, which means they can plan ahead. Plus, they get to answer the telephones and shout out orders to the rest of us. Most of them don't work on the weekends, and rarely do they have to throw away a new dress shirt because of blood or mud stains. The custodian, along these same lines, claims a certain tacit power, power that comes from the other employees' fearful care of not tracking in red mud or dropping flower petals on freshly vacuumed carpets. Despite his firmly fixed position at the bottom of the rung, the guy who cuts the grass and washes the cars is pretty much his own boss; as long as he keeps the yard freshly shorn and the vehicles crisp and clean, nobody bothers him. The funeral directors have a license, a two-year degree from an accredited mortuary college, and a title to support their elevation on the ladder. The owner? Well, that's the name on the sign out front. You don't get much higher than that.

That leaves the funeral assistants. "Funeral men," as they are often called, make up the bulk of the human resource pool in most funeral homes in the South. And the majority of these assistants are either college students plodding through a part-time job or retirees who want to get away from their wives for a few hours each day. Some of these funeral men are actually women. Ah, times are a 'changing. A few funeral assistants are people without the credentials to be licensed who have decided to work in the death care industry as their full-time jobs.

A small subclass of the funeral assistant consists of apprentices. Apprenticeships in this country have not generally enjoyed a positive reputation, thanks in part to tales like Benjamin Franklin's *The Autobiography* in which Franklin details the horrors of being apprenticed to his printmaker brother, or Donald Trump's *Celebrity Apprentice* where the Donald yells at people before shouting, "You're fired!"

My beginnings in the funeral business started somewhere in the middle of the lower end of the hierarchy; I was twenty-three years old and a recent college graduate with a lot of hollow self-confidence that came from a freshly minted bachelor's degree crammed into my top dresser drawer; my death care ignorance, on the other hand, relegated me to the status of grunt level funeral assistant, and I use the word assistant loosely.

I was apprenticed to an embalmer named Arnold Maddox. A Vietnam War veteran with the temperament of a house-cat (amiable one minute and ready to claw out your eyeballs the next), just about everybody called him Arnie. Arnie took me under his wing, and underneath the crotchety veneer of stories from the good ol' days and a half century's worth of sandpaper sarcasm, I found a guy who knew a lot about embalming and even more about human nature. Arnie taught me everything there was to know about the world of arteries, veins, trocars, and aneurism hooks. It was Arnie who, while embalming a woman who had undergone the indignity of an autopsy, proved to me that, yes indeed, we all do look the same on the inside.

"You're an apprentice, so whenever an embalmer is in the preparation room, you need to be there apprenticing."

"I thought I was apprenticed to you," I said innocently.

Arnie sighed. "And I'm telling you that you need to be in here helping whenever you're not on a funeral, even if that somebody you're helping's not me."

And that was how I ended up in the embalming room with Myron. Myron was even older than Arnie. He looked like an embalmer. Short and thin, Myron made up for his lack of stature with a shock of snow white hair thicker than shag carpet. He was a gentleman through and through, though, his dark trousers, long-sleeve white shirt, and spotless tie always clean and pressed. When he embalmed, Myron liked to wear a white lab coat he'd had for ages. Even that old lab coat was spotless.

Every embalmer I've ever worked with has a unique way of doing things. Arnie reminded me all the time that my job was to do whatever the embalmer told me to do without question, and I never forgot it. In fact, Arnie and I worked together so long that I could predict what he was going to say before he said it, sort of like an old married couple. Myron, by stark contrast, was not at all predictable. He went about the task of embalming as if he were tearing down a shed – knock out some nails, pull the old clapboard, make a pile; Arnie, on the other hand, reminded me of a high school biology teacher when he embalmed. He wanted me to learn, and he expected me to listen, but I could tell sometimes that he felt ill-at-ease around me. Around Myron I was jumpy, sort of like a puppy trying to get a closer look at a pissed-off snake.

I stood out of Myron's way while he worked, but I could see that he knew what he was doing from the other side of the room, and to be honest, I was glad to get a look at how somebody else handled the dreadful arts. Myron made the small incision just above the right collar bone – a cut no longer than a paperclip. He pulled his way through tissue and muscle until he had the jugular vein and the carotid artery exposed and tied off with waxed string. While he worked, I tried to inch closer and pass him the implements of his trade that I thought he might need next, but he wasn't like Arnie; no, Myron did not want my interference, even to pass him a pair of hemostats.

That was why I was surprised when Myron requested my assistance.

"Get me the bone."

I just stood there. For months I had worked alongside Arnie in the embalming room. I had learned my way around the tables and cabinets and shelves. I had located and procured autopsy needles, eye caps, trocar buttons, head blocks, arm rests, scalpel blades, toe tags, razors, combs, fingernail polish, "suntan" makeup, lipstick, white powder, tinted powder, hand soap, body soap, fingernail files, nail trimmers, cotton balls, cotton fabric, panty hose, knee highs, all types of underwear, bottles of embalming fluid, bottles of cavity fluid, white sheets, white hand towels, body bags, and even a plastic milk jug; but not once in my tenure as an embalmer's apprentice had I been sent in search of the bone.

"The what?"

"The bone, the bone," Myron growled. "You know the bone. I need the bone."

No, I didn't know the bone. No one had ever instructed me to get a bone. What kind of bone did he want? In an embalming room, a request for a bone is loaded with awful implications. I had seen bodies arrive in which broken bones were clearly visible. Sometimes the bones, usually covered in skin, tissue, and muscle, were not even attached to the bodies.

There were bones that had been stripped of their protective covers so that they stuck out white and foreign against whatever was left of bodies. In all those instances, though, no one ever asked me to get one.

"Myron, I don't know what you're talking about."

He looked at me, his face contorted in a jumble of old age and disgust. My father gave me that same look when I told him that I wanted to take a year off between high school and college to get my bearings. He'd told me that I wasn't old enough for my bearings to be any place other than where they were supposed to be, and that I wasn't going to waste a year of my life sitting around the house.

Myron pushed past me and walked to the drawer that held the miscellany of embalming utensils. He dug, pushed, threw, and mumbled. Finally, from the back of the drawer beneath the faded green instrument tray, he found it – the bone. "This is the bone," he said, holding it up to my face. "It's officially called the Bone Separator."

What he showed me was indeed a bone, a whittled down piece of osseous matter about six inches long, an inch and a half wide, and not much thicker than a slice of turkey.

"Is that a real bone?"

"Of course, it is," snarled Myron. "It's a deer bone. I bet you thought I wanted something used to actually separate a bone. You young people need to go to embalming school."

"What's it used for?"

Myron pushed past me again, walked over to the body lying on the table, and slipped the bone underneath the raised artery and vein. "It holds up the vessels," he said.

I learned early on that most embalmers share a common practice when draining a lifeless body of blood: building up pressure. In most cases, embalming fluid is pumped into the carotid artery, and that pressure forces blood out through the jugular vein. In this manner, the copper-scented blood is removed from a body and replaced with embalming fluid. To aid with drainage, many embalmers start the process of pumping the fluid into the artery, only to wait a little while before sliding back the stopper in the drain tube to get the blood flowing red and river-like. Arnie usually waited twenty or thirty seconds before he opened the drain tube. But not Myron.

At just over a minute, Myron had yet to relieve the pressure to start drainage. The vein was beginning to swell and a thin rivulet of blood was bubbling from the incision.

"Um, Myron, do you think you should release the drain tube?"

Without looking down at the body, Myron turned to me. For the record, let me state that I did my best to bring this situation to Myron's attention in the most tactful, the most respectful voice possible. Myron, however, failed to appreciate my efforts.

"Young man," he said, his voice airy and nasally as though too much oxygen escaped each time he opened his mouth to speak, "I've been embalming bodies for forty-five years."

While he spoke, I watched the vein begin to swell even more.

"I owned my own funeral home in Virginia before I moved here, and I didn't need no college boy telling me how to do my job then, and I don't appreciate you coming into my preparation room and giving me orders now."

By that point I had begun to back up toward the door. Not only was the visible vein swelling beyond its breaking point, but the flesh around the incision had started to protrude.

"Don't you walk away from me while I'm talking to you," Myron spat as I opened the embalming room door. "Young man, this is something you need to hear. Might bring you down a notch or two."

At that moment I heard it – a pop – a soft, muffled pop like the sound of a bubble-gum bubble popping behind your tongue. Myron, who was standing over the body and the engorged vein, had his eyes on me when the drain tube blew, but he heard it, too. A geyser of red and pink exploded into the air, covering Myron's hair, face, and clothes. I think his mouth might have been open.

The old embalmer, his arms out and his palms pointed up in a position of majestic supplication, looked at me; blood and embalming fluid dripped from his white hair, traced the lines down his face, and spattered onto his lab coat. In his eyes I saw pleading, but there was nothing I could do.

"Well, don't just stand there. Get me a towel!"

"Myron, you've been embalming for forty-five years," I said as I left the room. "And only forty-five years of experience can handle this mess."

Death

Caved and Dented

Oftentimes, the funerals we worked were merely the conclusions to longer, more complicated narratives. Worn out families, families forced to admit failures, found themselves staring at lifeless faces in awful caskets. Standing there, many of the heartbroken asked themselves the universal question – Why? And quite often the answers ended up being more complex than any of us cared to acknowledge. Too many times, though, the answers were as simple as the litany of human sins: lust, gluttony, greed, sloth, wrath, envy, pride. Here's one of those backstories.

When she found the note in his pants pocket, all she could do was laugh through the tears. She knew better than to have married a man like him. Her mama spotted that early on, back when they were high-school sweeties. Now a love note, but not from her – from some stranger.

"Go play outside," she told the little girl.

"But, Mommy, I want to be with you and Daddy. When's Daddy coming home?"

"Just go on outside."

The wife waited on the sofa, the smoke from her cigarette forming haloes above her head. The husband smelled of sweat and grease when he walked through the front door from work, and she found herself disgusted by what she'd once found so familiar.

"What's this?" she asked, the paper crumpling between her fingers.

He read the note and stuffed it into his pants pocket.

"How could you?"

He turned and walked into the other room. In the tiny kitchen, his dirty hand rested on the table.

"How could I what?"

She moved toward him. "I gave you everything, my whole life! And what do you do? You cheat on me with some trash! Why her? Wasn't I good enough for you?"

He sighed. This was not at all what he'd wanted, any of it.

She struck his face with her open hand, but he made no move to defend himself. His cheek felt hot and scratchy against her skin.

"Feel better?" he asked, and he rolled his tongue along the inside of his cheek.

"Get out of my house!"

He pushed past her, knocking her against the kitchen table. Last Halloween's pumpkin fell to the floor with a thump.

"Don't touch me!" she cried.

The small squeak the little girl's toy made when he tread upon it was a slight noise, not even big enough really for him to notice. But he looked down at the doll anyway, its chest caved and its head dented from the heel of his boot. A minute later he reemerged from the bedroom with a black plastic bag containing clothes, toothbrush, and a color photograph.

"I'm sorry," the husband whispered from the doorway.

"Don't say that to me!"

"What do you want to hear, then?"

"I don't want to hear anything! I want you to be the husband you vowed you'd be!"

"I'm a jerk. I know it. It's just who I am."

Through her tears she saw him going. Porch. Steps. Yard.

"I hate you! I'm sorry I ever met you!"

He felt compassion for the woman he loved. He whispered. "Go back inside. You're embarrassing yourself."

"Me? You're the one who broke your promise! You're the one who should be embarrassed."

Such anger. This woman, this wife, who wouldn't let him just go.

No further words were necessary, so he jumped into his old truck. The seat felt good against his back, and for a moment he could have closed his eyes and drifted to someplace far-away. He slapped the radio button, and Johnny Cash crooned the words to "Daddy." The wife descended the steps, her arms waving, her mouth moving in a noiseless pantomime. He turned up the volume.

Hysterical. She didn't want him to leave. That was it. She wanted to berate him until there was nothing left but ham-mered flesh. He just wanted to get the hell out of there. He pulled the gearshift to reverse.

"Stop!" her heard her yell over the music.

Anger, thick and hot. Johnny Cash kept singing.

He stomped the gas and the truck lurched backward. A soft thud, like the sound a pumpkin makes when it falls off a kitchen table. A strange sensation – cottony and light – be-neath the weight of the truck. A small squeak. A child's toy?

The wife dropped to the ground in front of him, her hands covering her open mouth. He kicked open the door and fell into the dirt. There lay his little girl, his doll. Her chest caved. Her head dented.

"Daddy."

Elvis Has Left the Building

I met Kenny Rucker on my second day working at the funeral home. The ice from a recent winter storm still littered the ground – finger-size fragments that had fallen from limbs high in the oaks and elms surrounding the property – and Kenny was busy sweeping the front walkway.

"You the new guy they just hired." It was more of a statement than a question, a subtle point to make me aware that he knew more than most people expected.

I let the front door close behind me, and a gust of cold air blew up my pants legs. "Good morning, I'm …"

"I know your name." He switched the long-handle push broom to his left hand and extended his right. "I'm Kenny. Everybody just calls me Elvis."

"Elvis? Why Elvis?"

He grinned a mouthful of straight, white teeth. "Oh, I don't know, man. I guess it's my poufy black hair and country twang." He laughed. "Those boys you workin' with gave me that nickname a couple years ago. They sure are some weird dudes. Especially Arnie. You on his shift, right?"

"Yep."

"Yeah, Arnie used to be a mortician in the army. Watch his temper, though. That man throws a fit about once a week."

I'd seen one of Arnie's fits the day before. Somebody left a used scalpel blade on the counter in the preparation room, and I thought he was going to pop an artery the way he stomped around and threw stuff everywhere.

"What all do you do here?"

"Well, I make sure the cars are clean and shiny, and I cut the grass and rake the leaves. That and keeping the basement clean takes about all my time."

I had already noticed that the flower van had to be the cleanest vehicle in town: sparkling rims, dust-free dash, and not a flower petal, dried up or otherwise, to be found in the cargo area. I looked over at the hearse Elvis had pulled out in front of the chapel. Even with the muddy puddles, decaying leaves, and melting ice, the hearse looked like somebody had just driven it off the showroom floor.

"How long you been here?"

"About three years." He resumed his sweeping. "I like it here. Everybody's real nice."

"I hope I like it."

"You on a good shift; you'll like it."

There were three shifts. Arnie, Clyde Combs, and I were now on one. Coy Franklin, Delbert Floyd, and Lester Polk on another. Hoke Harris headed up the third shift, but I hadn't met the other two men yet.

I turned to go back down to the preparation room to help Arnie as Elvis swept his way on down the sidewalk.

Elvis, I later found out, lived about three miles from the funeral home in a loft apartment in one of the old textile mill villages.

"Here," Arnie said, and he thrust a set of keys into my right hand and an address scrawled across a scrap of paper into the other. "Take the Ford van and go pick up Elvis."

I read the address and realized that I knew the street; it ran right in front of a Pentecostal Holiness church where we'd had a service not two weeks earlier. "And why am I picking him up?"

Arnie pointed toward the four panes in the garage door. Beyond the windows the March rain pounded the parking lot. "Elvis doesn't have a driver's license, and he called and asked one of us to come get him so he doesn't have to walk in the rain. Now go get him. We all got stuff to do."

"How about let's stop and pick up some supplies on the way back in," said Elvis after he climbed into the front seat.

I watched as two small hands waved goodbye from the upstairs window.

"Your children?" I asked.

"Yeah. A boy and a girl."

Elvis pointed the way through narrow streets I had yet to learn toward the little hardware store. As we rode along, the rhythm of the rain lulling both of us into a happy daze, I thought about Elvis.

"So, why don't you have a driver's license?"

Elvis laughed. "Boy, you don't beat around the bush, do you?"

"Sorry," I said. "I didn't mean to pry."

"Oh, no. It's all right." He wiped his hands on his pants and pushed himself back into the seat. "Alcohol," he said matter-of-factly. "Lost my license after my second DUI."

"Oh."

"'Oh' is right." After a long pause, he continued. "How old

you think I am?"

I looked to my right and gave a quick study of his face. "I don't know. Forty maybe."

"Forty-one," he admitted. "Forty-one years old last October. And I ain't done a single thing with my life besides get married, have a couple of kids, and get into trouble."

I heard my grandmother's voice in my head. "It's never too late to start over."

"Oh, I know that. Sure I do. It's just that a man starts to regret the choices he made when he was younger, and the fix seems so easy lookin' back."

We pulled into the parking lot, and I watched him hop out and head into the cinder-block building. Elvis was a short man, barely five and a half feet tall. His tight curly black hair was already backing away from his forehead, and his skin was deep and dark. I could tell that the years had been hard on him. But that smile just spread across his face as if he hadn't a care in the world. I knew then that I liked working with him.

By the time he returned to the van with an armful of cleaners and disinfectants, the rain had darkened his green uniform. "Whew," he chuckled. "It's wetter than water out there."

After our brief talk, I began to notice Elvis a little more. Quiet and hard-to-rile, he possessed the decisive confidence of a rich man. He completed his work each day without anyone staying on him to get the job done, and when his outside duties were finished, he came underground to the basement to tackle the manmade messes.

He knew he was at the bottom of the funeral home ladder, working a job that had no real capacity for vertical movement. But he didn't seem to mind. Always humming a tune I could never quite place, he went about the day's business as if nothing else mattered. Years later, I would hear my father-in-law mention that his daily objective was to complete all tasks as if he were working for Jesus himself. That was Elvis, happily fulfilling his duties at the funeral home, working toward some loftier goal than a mere paycheck or human recognition.

Early one morning on a day with no funerals, Elvis tapped me on the shoulder. "Uh, Coy wants you and me to clean the selection room."

The selection room was where families picked out caskets. The twenty-five-by-fifty-foot room, complete with a low ceiling and unflattering lighting, was the last place people wanted to find themselves. Surrounded by roughly thirty caskets back in those days, walking into the room proved to be a shock for most people, and Elvis was no different.

"I just don't like it in here," muttered Elvis. His eyes scanned the walls. "Nope, they didn't hire me for this kind of work. Hearses and limousines I can take, but not caskets."

The kind of work Elvis was referring to was me moving caskets while he vacuumed around, under, and behind them. "It shouldn't take too long," I said.

He shook his head slightly and looked up at the ceiling. "Any time in here is too long, so let's get to it."

We worked for a good hour, me in my slacks, white shirt, and tie, moving the caskets here and there so Elvis could vacuum.

"Why you reckon people want to spend so much money on a casket they just gonna cover up with dirt?" Elvis asked during a quick break.

I hadn't been there long enough to formulate a real opinion, so I had to think about that question. "I don't know, really."

"Guilt," he said. "Guilt."

"What do you mean?"

He pointed toward a beautiful silver hinge-cap, the official name was Empire, made by the Toccoa Casket Company out of Toccoa, Georgia. "You take that casket there. Coy and Hoke sell that one or the Ambassador all the time. But why don't people just buy this little cloth-covered cheap one over here?" He didn't wait for my response. "Because Grandma's getting old and she's been feeling poorly for some time, and now the children and grandchildren see that they've been neglecting her. Now that she's dead, they feel real guilty and want to buy her something nice for the sendoff." He shrugged. "Guilt."

I thought back to a psychology course I'd taken in college, and what Elvis said made sense. "Okay, so if Coy and Hoke know that everybody's going to buy the Empire or the Ambassador, why do we have so many caskets to choose from?"

He looked around the room. I saw his eyes fall on the John, the one with "The Last Supper" on it. "I don't know. Maybe because variety is the spice of life." Elvis smiled. "No, I'm kidding. We're required to keep a certain number of caskets. Okay, back to work. I don't want to be in here any longer than I have to."

We made our way, casket-by-casket, across the selection room, leaving a fresh pattern in the carpet as a testament to our labors. We were all the way in the back corner, just about to tackle the last few square yards of floor, when the lights flickered.

Elvis let go of the vacuum cleaner and cocked his head to the side. "What was that?"

"I don't know."

We waited another moment or two, and when nothing else happened, Elvis started breathing again and fired up the vacuum cleaner while I pulled the Presidential Mahogany away from the corner. Just then the room went black. No flicker. No warning. Just complete darkness. Because the selection room was in the basement, there were no windows, and that was the darkest dark I'd ever found myself in.

People say that the loss of one sense can throw the others into overdrive. While I don't know the science behind such claims, there must be something to it. In his frantic attempt to find daylight, Elvis ran toward the door, knocking the vacuum cleaner over and slamming into several caskets.

"Hey, you all right?" I yelled in the darkness.

I heard him jerk open the selection room door and pound down the hallway toward the back door and the parking lot. When I finally picked my way through the darkness, Elvis was nowhere in sight.

"Why was Elvis running down James Street?" Clyde Combes asked.

"The power went out while we were vacuuming the selection room. It was pretty dark."

"He doesn't like being in the dark," Lester Polk reminded us. "Yes, sir. He's always been a little particular about where he goes in the funeral home. But now the dark – he hates the dark worse than anything else." Lester turned around and headed back inside. "Yep, ol' Elvis has left the building again."

"Elvis has left the building," became a catchall statement whenever any of us might be looking for Elvis and couldn't find him.

"It's almost 5:30," somebody would say. "Elvis has already left the building."

His wife called. "Elvis has left the building."

We needed help with a particularly messy situation in the preparation room. "Not gonna happen. Elvis has left the building."

Kenny "Elvis" Rucker and I ended up working a lot together. I finally met his wife and children. Listened to stories about his parents. Heard more than once how he hoped for a way to make a better life for his family.

One day during my third year, I noticed that Elvis didn't show up for work one morning and he didn't call for a ride.

"You seen Elvis?" I asked Arnie.

"He quit."

"Quit?"

"Yep. Said he got another job."

And just like that, Elvis was gone.

Funeral home work attracts some interesting people, no doubt about that. I learned as much about people during my funeral home years as I did teaching high school. Elvis was one-of-a-kind. Humble, quiet, more intelligent than most people assumed, Elvis had a plan for his life, and he wasn't going to let a bunch of wisecracking undertakers deter him.

For some of us, the funeral home served as one of life's many layovers, a necessary stopping point along the way. So it was with Elvis. Clyde Combs said he went on to work in a bakery on the other side of town. Delbert Floyd heard Elvis was a preacher in Greenville. Either way, after teaching me more about life than I realized, Elvis had finally left the building.

Making the Removal

Blest Be the Man

Shift work can be soul-draining work. Anybody who's ever worked long shifts day after day understands the inescapable monotony that comes after too many shifts without a change of pace. The funeral business is really no different. Arnie and I worked a shift with another man, Clyde Combs. Back in those days, three three-man shifts kept a set three-week schedule. On the nights Arnie, Clyde, and I took call, Clyde and I spent the night in the apartment on the second floor of the funeral home; the two of us lived too far out of town to be able to get back to the funeral home in a hurry should we receive a death call in the middle of the night.

Because I was the youngest and a freshly registered apprentice, I answered the telephone and took the death calls. This was the time before somebody had the bright idea to turn over the night shift to the answering service. Some nights the phone never rang; other nights, I'm not sure I got any sleep at all. Arnie lived about five miles away, and he had already left for the night. Clyde had showered, changed into his pajamas, and was brushing his teeth by the time I turned out all the lights in all the state rooms and made my way up the stairs to the outdated apartment.

"Nighty-night," Clyde called as he disappeared inside the cluttered bedroom he called his own every third night.

I walked into the big bedroom, the one with the telephone, and flipped on the bedside lamp. My queen-size bed looked inviting, but I needed to clean up before turning in; it had been a long, hot day. By the time I pulled back the covers, it was nearly 11:30. I yawned, turned off the lamp, and fell asleep before the light bulb got cold.

I remember being ripped from a restful slumber by the un-nerving sound of a ringing telephone.

"Great," I muttered before I picked up the handset. "Yes, ma'am. Yes, ma'am. That's off Highway 81? Yes, ma'am, I'm pretty sure we can find it. We'll be right there."

My first order of business after taking a night-time death call was to call Arnie. He was the embalmer; Clyde and I were merely his apprentices – unlicensed funeral men. Too many nights, though, Clyde disappeared and went back to bed after we got back to the funeral home.

"Hello."

"We've got one."

"Who's dead?"

"Mr. Percy Murray. It's a house call."

"Hospice?"

"Yes."

"Bye."

Arnie walked through the door about fifteen minutes later, his tie hanging crooked and the fat knot cutting into his Adam's apple making his face redder than usual. His shirt was half buttoned and his index finger held his blue suit coat over his right shoulder.

"Whose turn is it?" he asked.

"You and me."

"Let me get presentable."

I backed the hearse out of the garage just a little before 1 AM. Arnie sat quietly in the passenger seat, his mass of wavy blond hair slicked down and no longer standing on end and his clothes more or less in good order.

"Where are we going?"

"Shakespeare Lane. It's just off 81 South."

There were basically three types of calls that we received in the middle of the night: hospital, nursing home, or house. Hospital calls were simple: show up, pick up, and back up. We didn't really need to concern ourselves with speed when we went to the hospital morgue. The only person we usually saw was the security guard who met us at the back door, and in the wee hours of the morning, he was most likely in a hurry to get back to his chair and his coffee. Nursing home calls required a little more haste in getting there, but half the time the only people there were a few close family members and a nurse or two. Nursing home calls took a bit longer once we got there, but most of the time the process was smooth.

House calls, on the other hand, were an entirely different proposition. Who knew what we would find on a house call? There could be five people waiting at the house; there could be fifty-five people. Mean dogs lurked behind trees. Babies cried. Directions turned out to be wrong. What we did know, though, was that we needed to get to the house as quickly as possible. The deceased could have passed away only minutes before the call, or the deceased could have been dead for hours. Our desire was never to leave the family waiting or create further anxiety for them.

Shakespeare Lane off Highway 81 South was a misnomer at best. I envisioned a thoroughfare, a lane no less, named after one of the world's most prolific playwrights to be something special, a pathway of poetic proportions that led to the most exclusive of finely manicured lawns and gardens, purposeful areas of grass and shrub that surrounded quaint homes possessing a thorough attention to design. I was an English major in college, and I had read my share of the Bard's work. I knew he had been married to a woman named Anne Hathaway and that his children were Susanna, Judith, and Hamnet. He was the principal playwright for the Lord Chamberlain's Men, and he made the Globe Theatre synonymous with name Shakespeare itself. On his grave appear the words "Blest be the man who spares these stones/Cursed be he that disturbs these bones." That pretty much sums it up for a funeral director.

The Shakespeare Lane we found that night, to my disappointment, turned out to be nothing like the Elizabethan pathway I'd envisioned. Orange clay packed hard, this particular Shakespeare Lane had been rutted to a washboard effect by running rainwater and speeding cars. Mobile homes lined both sides of the road, and there wasn't more than a slightly green space of a dozen feet between each of them. The windows in most of the houses were pitch black, not even a security light protecting the yards. But about seven trailers down on the right, a yellow glow caught my eye. Every light in the place was on, and a fire roared inside a rusty fifty-gallon drum some twenty feet from the house. Cars littered the yard; several sat sideways in the ditch. People milled about, cigarettes dangling from their lips or their fingers. I'm pretty sure I saw light from the porch reflect off numerous beer bottles.

"Oh, my," Arnie said.

"I agree."

I parked the hearse in what space was left in the crowded driveway. Arnie liked to leave the hearse running in case we needed to make a fast getaway – from what, he never told me – so I left the key in the ignition and got out.

We passed through the smoky yard, nodded our respectful acknowledgment of each family member or friend we met, and ascended the steps to the front deck. Because we had just emerged from a gloomy hearse and wore dark suits, who we were was not a mystery. Finding out who was in charge of this group, though, was not turning out to be an easy task: no one talked to us, and most of the people avoided any eye contact.

"Who's the next of kin?" Arnie asked.

I pulled the first call sheet from my pocket. "Shelia Murray, the wife. I talked with the Hospice nurse, Pam."

"Shelia or Pam," I heard Arnie mutter to himself as he pulled open the complaining storm door.

Arnie, while a competent embalmer and funeral director who took his craft seriously, sometimes turned to mush around live people. He had worked so long in the embalming room with folks who hardly ever created a fuss that when he did get out among the living, he tended to freeze up. His palms grew sweaty and his already ruddy face got even redder. He was prone to mumble and fidget like a schoolgirl on a first date, and I could see that his discomfort had already gotten the better of him that night.

"Want me to do the talking?"

"I've got it."

Pam met us in the crowded living room. "Mr. Murray is in the last room down the hallway to the right," she said. "And this is Mrs. Murray."

Arnie extended a hand to the grieving widow standing in the shadows. "My name is Arnie." He pointed to me, but he seemed to have forgotten my name. "This is, um..., uh..., we're here to make the removal."

Mrs. Murray obviously did not understand the word removal, and her present sorrow would have muddled her brain had she known what Arnie meant. She looked at Arnie, then to Pam, then to me.

"We're going to take Mr. Murray back to the funeral home," I said.

Mrs. Murray smiled. "Oh, yes." And then she began to cry.

"Have you had enough time with Mr. Murray?" Arnie asked. "You know, before we go on back to the funeral home?"

The tears came like a fountain. "Yes. Y'all go ahead and get him." She turned and started walking down the narrow hallway in the opposite direction from the room where her husband lay a corpse. "If you have any other questions, you can talk to my son, Gene. He's outside."

Before Arnie could say anything else, Mrs. Murray disappeared into a sea of people, cigarette smoke, and two-liter Mountain Dews.

"I'll show you where he is," Pam offered.

The bedroom was dark. It smelled stale, as if sickness and death had lingered so long that the two inexorable predicaments became one. Two women stood on either side of the bed, the tears streaking their faces visible in the pale light of a lone corner lamp.

"This is Mr. Murray's daughters," said Pam.

Arnie and I acknowledged the women, and before we could say anything, Pam spoke up. "They're here to take your daddy to the funeral home now."

As if they unquestioningly conceded authority to nurses and funeral directors, the women turned and left the room without so much as a word to interrupt their weeping. We went back to the hearse, retrieved the cot, and then collected Mr. Murray.

By the time we left the bedroom, the living room had filled up with people, smoke, and loud talk. Just about everyone quieted down, while a few of the more inebriated of the bunch kept on laughing in the kitchen. We pushed our way through the swarm and out into the damp chill of night. Softly, tenderly, we pointed our cot toward the yard. With as much grace as we could manage after teetering down the steep wooden steps and bumping our way along the chunky gravel driveway, we slid Mr. Murray into the cavernous opening at the back of the hearse.

"Dang," Arnie whispered.

"What?"

"I forgot to get permission to embalm."

In South Carolina, funeral directors need verbal permission from the family before beginning the process of embalming.

"You want me to do it?"

"Let's go," was all he said.

We began our slow retreat back to the house. Both of us, remembering Mrs. Murray's desire that any further issues be dealt with through her son, scanned the available bystanders for someone who could be the son. Several men loitered beneath a sorry-looking Bradford pear, smoking and talking quietly. Two men holding beer bottles hovered near the front steps with three women. Three more men sat on the tailgate of a pickup truck, their legs dangling and thin.

"Excuse me," Arnie said to a man standing in the doorway of the trailer. "Can you tell me where I can find Mr. Murray's son? I believe his name is Gene."

The man looked out through red, watery eyes. The pores of his skin exuded the stale odor of alcohol, and the cigarette sticking out of his mouth was just before dropping its three inches of ripe ash. His head had so recently been shorn that his slick pate glistened in the moonlight.

"I'm Gene."

Arnie extended his hand. "My name's Arnie, and this is… um…uh… We're from the funeral home."

"I know where you're from."

I could sense Arnie's anxiety, but there was little I could do. As the junior man, I stayed out of the way until needed.

Gene's far-away expression zoomed in on Arnie, and the tension in the air seemed to radiate out so that even people standing nearby hushed their conversations for an earful of what might follow. Apparently Gene had a reputation, and the emotions a man's brain can summon must have rushed in on him tidal-wave-like, working together with an already fitful temper and the ingestion of something alcoholic to bring this brief encounter to a head.

"Well, we need to know if we can embalm it when we get back to the funeral home," Arnie said.

I heard the pronoun confusion, and I know Gene heard it, though I doubt he had any clue what a pronoun was. All he heard was *it*.

"My daddy ain't no damned *it!*" he yelled, and I thought for a moment that Gene might actually hit Arnie.

I stepped up, awkwardly and openly circumventing the long-established pecking order, and put my hand on Gene's shoulder. "He didn't mean anything by that," I said. "It's late, everybody's tired. We know your daddy's not an *it*. Your daddy was a good man, and I know you all loved him."

Gene turned around and spat into the grass. "He was a son of a bitch if there ever was one," he said. "Y'all go ahead and get him out of here and do your embalming."

He pushed past us and joined a couple of mouth-breathing locals standing by a split open dogwood tree. "Somebody give me a beer," we heard Gene say.

Arnie and I walked back down the stairs into the yard. The hearse waited for us only fifteen feet away, but I know it felt like fifteen miles for poor old Arnie. Once inside the safety of the front seat, I heard Arnie sigh. I was backing the hearse onto the narrow dirt road when Arnie chuckled.

"Who was it that said 'Blessed be the man who doesn't mess up his pronouns'?"

I grinned and looked at the street sign about to fall off its post. "I think it was Shakespeare."

Taking Your Work Home

The temperature climbed to 95 degrees before lunchtime, just the same as it had every day for a fortnight. By 3:00 in the afternoon, even a shady spot felt like a pizza oven with the temperature topping out at over one hundred and staying there until dark. Birds failed to sing; insects kept quiet. The air hung heavy with dust and sweat, and the energy-zapping heat made it an August to remember. I wish that was the only remarkable part of that summer.

Off by itself down an orange, powdery dirt road, the old mobile home hunched on its cement block foundation. An ambulance, a sheriff's deputy's car, and a beat-up Ford pickup truck with a Dale Earnhardt bumper sticker waited in the yard. The grass had died some time ago, and the brown stubble that was left looked ready to poof into ashes at little more than a warm fart. Two EMTs, a man and a woman wearing black BDUs and blue short-sleeve work shirts, the deputy in his black uniform, and a short man scratching under his cowboy hat who I assumed was the coroner stood dead-man still underneath a parched water oak out from the house. Their serious expressions could have meant a thousand things, but for us, they bore only one implication of any importance: Whatever was waiting on us inside that trailer was not going to be good.

"This could be interesting," Arnie said.

I pulled the hearse beside the ambulance and shifted to park. "Yep."

Out of habit, I grabbed a pack of latex rubber gloves and shoved them into my coat pocket. The full force of the heat belted me in the face when I opened the hearse door, and beads of perspiration instantly popped out onto my forehead and nose.

Arnie and I both eyed the brown and white trailer as we walked across the yard. The front door was closed, and the windows, blacked out and covered, seemed to shimmer in the August heat.

"Afternoon," said the coroner. "I'm Red Shiflet."

"Glad to know you, Red." Arnie stuck out his hand. "I'm Arnie Maddox; this is um, ah….We're from the funeral home."

Mr. Shiflet pulled a piece of paper out of his shirt pocket, unfolded it, and scanned it with foggy eyes. "Here. This has everything you need to know about the deceased on it."

He handed the paper to Arnie. "Bill Hall," Arnie read. A common name for a common existence.

"That's right," said the coroner. "He was under a doctor's care. Liver cancer. He was supposed to be moved to the Hospice House two weeks ago, but he refused. Said he wanted to die at home. He died by himself."

Arnie shook his head. "If that's what he wanted."

"We're through on our end," Red informed us. "Y'all are welcome to go ahead and get him."

"Any family around?" Arnie asked.

"Nobody local," Red replied. "He was it. Got a daughter down in Jacksonville who says for y'all to go ahead and get him, that she'll be on up in a couple of days."

A miserable black dog walked up from behind the trailer, stopped, sniffed, and turned around and trotted off in the other direction. Without thinking, I sniffed. Just below the smell of dirt in the dense heat, a strange odor lingered. It was gamey and raw and ready to explode.

The EMTs came over to where we stood. We recognized both of them.

"I thought you guys usually brought the bodies to us in cases like this," quipped Arnie with a smile.

The woman, I think her name was Rusty, shook her head. "Not today, fellows. This one's all yours."

The male EMT grinned as the two of them started to walk away. "We'll be glad to help you if you want us to. You just holler."

"What you boys got in the way of protective clothing?" Red asked.

I pulled the rubber gloves from my pocket.

He shook his head and blew a gust of air out his nose. "That might make a good start, but it ain't gonna get the job done."

"What do you mean?" asked Arnie.

"Y'all got yourselves any isolation suits?"

"We do."

"I got mine," Red said, and he reached into the back of his truck and took out a couple of plastic bags. "Y'all had best go ahead and get yourselves suited up, then."

"What happened to Mr. Hall?" I asked before I walked to the hearse to get some protective gear.

Red Shiflet pursed his lips before turning his head and spitting brown tobacco juice to the dehydrated yard. "Last time anybody saw Mr. Hall was Monday. Neighbor down the way said she saw him wandering around in the yard with that old dog over there. Said he was skin and bones and was having a hard time walking, and she watched him go into his house there about lunchtime."

Red took off his hat and shirt. He ripped open the plastic bags and took out the white coveralls with an attached hood, shoe covers, goggles, and heavy duty gloves. "Best we can figure it, he died sometime Monday. Looks like he went to sleep on his couch in the living room."

"Monday?" I heard myself say as I counted the five days since then and thought about the heat.

"He on the couch now?" asked Arnie.

"What's left of him."

"Was the air conditioner running when you found him?"

Red yanked the tight coveralls over his fleshy stomach and sagging dugs. "Afraid not."

I could feel myself sweating from every pore as I moved toward the door wearing that airtight cocoon of an isolation suit. My breath fogged up my goggles, and as stuffed up as I was in that suit, the stink still wiggled its way to my nose. The old cider block steps shifted under our weight as we climbed to the front door.

The dirty windows kept moving in the heat. But when I looked closer, I realized that the windows weren't as dirty as I'd thought, and that the movement came from thousands of blue flies. Even through the hood I could hear their buzzing.

"Are those flies?" Arnie asked.

Red pulled open the front door. "You ain't seen nothing, yet."

A stench unlike anything I could have ever imagined poured out the door. It was so bad that my eyes watered and I felt nauseous. I choked back the morning's toast and eggs, slowed my breathing, and followed Arnie and Red into the trailer. The living room was dark, for all the shades were pulled down. The floor crunched beneath our feet, and I realized that thousands of dead, bloated flies littered the carpet.

"My word, it's hot in here," Arnie said.

"One-hundred twenty eight degrees when we first got on scene," Red hollered so we could hear him. "Mr. Hall didn't turn on the air conditioner before he died. With it so hot, even at night, this place fired up just like an oven." He pointed to the couch. "That didn't help the body none."

The old couch sagged from the weight of its load. Someone had thrown a crisp white sheet over the body, but it, too, hung heavy so that dark, wet spots spread out across it like widening ripples of despair. The three of us stopped there looking at the sheet, and the faint outline of a long, thin body slowly emerged.

Arnie snorted. "We're not getting anything done just standing here. Let's see what we're up against."

He reached down to reveal the body, and I noticed that there appeared to be movement under the sheet, a slight, hardly perceptible movement as of someone breathing softly while sleeping. Focused and aware of himself, Arnie grasped the edge of the sheet with the thumb and index finger of his right hand and pulled back with all the anticipation of a man who wasn't quite sure what he would find, but all the while understanding the mandate for caution.

The sight I beheld that day remains forever seared into the deeper recesses of my mind. Five days of heat-fueled decomposition had freed the skull of much of its constricting muscles, tissue, and skin. Everything looked like it had simply melted off and to the sides in greasy piles. Underneath the clothing, I once again detected movement. The man's white, button-up, long-sleeve dress shirt and worn out blue jeans, while moist and heavy and dirty with so much of what had only recently been inside him, had helped to keep most of his body below the neck in-tact. Careful of where I stepped or what I touched, I leaned down for a closer inspection. Sure enough, the white shirt almost vibrated. I moved even closer; I was certain my eyes were playing tricks on me in the heat.

"Maggots," Red hollered beside me. "Look around you. They're everywhere."

All around us, maggots, fly larvae in various stages of life, wriggled and inched in and out of sight. They scurried sight-less out from underneath the body where they tumbled over the edge of the couch. Those on the floor weren't left with nothing, though. Some of the decomposing body had leaked down the side of the couch.

Arnie patted me on the shoulder. "Let's get our stuff."

By stuff, he meant the cot from the hearse and a body bag, maybe two body bags.

The air outside the mobile home came as a welcome relief. I lifted my goggles to the top of my head and pulled the hood to the side so I could breathe. We went back inside with the cot, the body bags, four bottles of absorbent embalming powder called Action, a bottle of glue, and a few more white winding sheets.

"Anything in the pockets we need to remove?" Arnie asked. "Any rings or jewelry to come off?"

Red Shiflet grinned behind his mask. "No jewelry, but I didn't think to check his pants pockets." He shook his head. "We'd better look for his billfold."

What he meant was that Arnie and I should look for the bill-fold. Arnie didn't have to tell me what to do. I stepped over and placed my hands on the dead man's hips. Arnie nodded that he was ready. Using the care one might afford a sleeping baby, I lifted slowly. The body was lighter than I expected. When I had the hips raised about five inches, Arnie reached between dead man and couch and patted his rear back pockets. Moving the body unleashed a new wave of smells, larvae, and liquid. With a nod of his head, Arnie signaled that he'd found something. I held that position another twenty seconds while Arnie worked the wallet out of the man's pocket.

Once Arnie pulled his arm out of harm's way, I lowered the body back to the couch. The wallet Arnie held out looked bloated, pretty much the way I figured the body may have been a couple of days earlier before the insects made their way through it, and I supposed its condition was a result of the leather and the paper soaking up the moisture.

"Drop it in here," Red said, holding out a clear evidence bag.

"Let's lay the body bag on the floor and open it up," Arnie said. "We'll see if we can get him into the first bag. We'll seal him inside and put that bag inside the second one."

That, so it seemed, might be easier said than done. To our surprise, the old sofa appeared to have a sheet draped across the top of it, and the deceased lay on top of the sheet. After covering the man back over, Arnie pulled up the corners around the head and feet. This was where we would grasp and lift.

My eyes filled with sweat, and flies buzzed around my face. Something tickled my chest under my shirt, and I wondered if a fly had gotten in. I thought I would get more used to the overpowering smell, but it was just the opposite: the nausea returned. Choking back the sick feeling rising in my throat made me cough, but I kept it all down.

Arnie wrapped the two ends of the sheet near the head around his left hand and grasped the gathered sheet folded over the torso of the dead man in his right hand. I followed his example on the other end of the body.

"Lift on three," he said. "One, two … three."

Sometimes a plan works flawlessly, as if it had been engineered for perfection from the start. And then there are the other times. We lifted the sheet together, careful to keep even pressure and our respective ends level. As soon as we had the sheet lifted about a foot above the couch and ready to move over toward the gaping black bag on the floor, the body started to move, and without the slightest noise, Mr. Hall's remains slipped through the sheet that separated like wet newspaper.

Arnie grunted and pointed to the floor. "Give me one of those sheets."

He opened the folded white sheet and handed an end to me. Ile didn't have to tell me what to do; I'd done it before. With the sheet pulled apart and flat, we made a single fold hot-dog style. Then another and another until we had it worked down to what looked like a seven-foot by six-inch strap. Arnie lifted the dead man's head and shoulders, and I looped the sheet around him just above his elbows. We made another impromptu strap and positioned this one beneath the man's legs just above his knees.

"Let's try it again," cautioned Arnie. "And careful this time."

Standing over the body, each of us lifted an end. After some shifting and bending, the body took to being raised hoist-style and cooperated. We backed up over the bag lying open on the floor, both of us on the body's right side, and gently laid the corpse atop the unzipped area.

"So far, so good," Arnie said with raised eyebrows.

We finagled the open edges of the bag around the legs first before working our way up the torso to the head and shoulders. I had to keep knocking away the maggots upset by the sudden movement and spilling restlessly out of the various openings.

We poured in the four bottles of moisture-absorbing powder.

Arnie tucked both sheets inside the bag and zipped it. "Pass me that bottle of glue."

He wiped the juices and maggots off the zipper as best he could before unscrewing the cap on a bottle of glue about the size of a small pickle jar. Attached to the inside of the cap was a paint brush, and Artie used short strokes to daub the sealant across the zipper and the adjacent fabric.

"Let's double bag him."

Using the black straps affixed to the bag, we lifted the full body bag and laid it on top of a new bag. Both of us now layered in our own sweat that seemed to soak up the smell of rotten death, we worked with the stiff material of the bags until the first bag was hidden inside the second one.

"Let's get the cot."

A crowd of neighbors and curiosity seekers stood in whatever shade they could find. My ears, dripping perspiration and obstructed by my protective hood, still picked up the subtle gasp that rose from the onlookers when we stepped out of the trailer.

I hated our return to the trailer of death. Inside, we lowered the cot to the floor and unfastened the straps. We placed the black body bag on the cot, and then we secured it with buckled straps. Arnie laid another clean white sheet over the body bag; I spread our plush black cot cover over the sheet. We were ready to go.

We used the hearse as cover while we peeled off our isolation suits. Even the sticky August air felt like a relief outside the impermeable coveralls. I reached for my coat, but Arnie shook his head.

"I know we're supposed to wear our suit coats in the hearse, but I think we can leave them off this once."

I smiled, nodded to Red Shiflet standing in the shade clad only in his white boxers, and closed the door. The conditioned air felt like heaven, and I could have gone to sleep right there.

We weren't five minutes from the funeral home when I felt something tickle my stomach. I reached inside my shirt and withdrew a faceless maggot.

"Those are hearty little critters," Arnie laughed. "I suppose you didn't think that one day you'd be pulling a maggot out of your belly button when they were handing you that college diploma, did you?"

"Never," I said, and I pondered my new wife's reaction to learning that part of her husband's day entailed the extrication of a plump, white maggot from his navel. No, I didn't need a college education to realize that some details of my life in the funeral home remained better off kept to myself.

A Death in the Family

The Jackson family sang together in church, and most people in town had listened to their harmonies at least once. When a distraught daughter called about 2:00 in the morning to tell me that her daddy had died, I felt a twinge of sympathy for a family I had already gotten to know as a result of their performances on funeral services.

"We'll be right there," I told the daughter.

The fog already hung heavy in the early morning hours of that Tuesday. The fog was so thick, in fact, that Arnie and I had trouble seeing out the hearse windows. I wondered if the weather was a sign of things to come.

On the ride out to the house, Arnie was quiet as usual. He probably hadn't fully waked up yet, which on most trips would be expected; on this night, though, Arnie decided that he wanted to drive. I kept one eye on him and the other on the road.

The inside of the pick-up hearse, an older model Sayers and Scoville Cadillac, felt like a deep airplane cockpit. As the rolling stock was updated every five or six years, the oldest funeral coach left in the refreshed pool found its way to the basement of the funeral home where people leaned against it, used the hood as a chair or table, bumped into it with cots and caskets, and often sat mouse-still in the shadowy front seat when they needed to hide from work. The bench seat was so low that the occupants up front had to strain to see past the broad, wide-as-a-school-desk dash. The interior didn't matter too much to folks in the back.

The glowing blue instrument panel spread across half the front. I imagined that the people watching us pass at night wondered what made our faces stand out azure against the eerie light. A good foot and a half above our heads, the ceiling domed out as a reminder of the funeral coach's evolutionary trek from buggy to ambulance to hearse. About as equally distinctive, but not as immediately noticeable by the motoring public, was the vehicle's smell. Somewhere between back-of-the-closet and dirty socks, the inside of the hearse reminded me that better times had already come and gone.

Virgil Jackson had spent thirty years with his wife and emerging family living out near the fairgrounds. They had lived in a grand Southern-looking home with a big front porch, high gables, and a shotgun hall, a house that harkened back to distant time before the surrounding neighborhood fell into disrepair. The paint on the outside of the house started peeling some years back, and most of it was gone; only the white streaks left in the cracks in the clapboards offered a glimpse of the house's healthier past.

Unlike other house calls, no one loitered in the yard or smoked by the weak yellow porch light. A couple of cars sat crammed into the black night of the back yard, but nothing testified to the unforeseen reality that the body of a living, breathing, laughing, crying human being now waited behind one of the heavy bedroom doors in icy solitude, the type of solitude that comes only with death.

We climbed the high steps to the front porch, the weather-weary floorboards creaking beneath our weight. Arnie cleared his throat, fidgeted with the choking knot of his necktie, and knocked on the tarnished screen door. A man sat still and quiet on the porch swing, his gaze high and lifted up over the tall treetops.

Arnie turned his head to the right and said, "Evening."

When the man left the greeting answerless, we figured he wanted to be by himself. Death does that to people. Both of us turned back toward the door when a slight woman appeared in the hallway and pushed open the door with her palm. She went about barefooted, her tiny feet shuffling across the hardwood floor.

"Yes?" she said.

"I'm Arnie, from the funeral home." Arnie nodded his head as if he wanted to bow but was afraid to. "And this is, um… He's from the funeral home, too."

"Glad to know you both," she said, peering past us into the foggy darkness. "My name's Lavinia. I'm married to Mr. Jackson's eldest son."

Lavinia directed us down the wide, gloomy hallway to a kitchen that shown white and glaring from the liberal use of too many hundred-watt light bulbs. Four people sat around a small table cradling cups of coffee, and a child played with a toy garbage truck over in the corner. An official-looking woman wearing starchy hospital scrubs motioned for us.

"I'm the Hospice nurse," she began, and she pointed to the people at the table. "This is Gladys Jackson, Mr. Jackson's wife. This is her daughter Rhonda, her other daughter Susan, and one of her sons, Ray. Her other son, Jimmy, is out of town and won't be back before tomorrow." She pointed toward the floor. "That's Jeremy, one of the great-grandchildren."

Arnie nodded and smiled to each family member. "I'm Arnie. This is, ah, um…We're from the funeral home."

While I wondered what it felt like to be the "other" daughter, I knew that we would forget all those names before we got back outside to the hearse.

And then it happened. Just like every other call I had ever been on, as soon as the introductions were made, we were forced to endure the long, unforgiving silence that followed. It seemed as if no one knew just what to say, for words come slowly and awkwardly when there's a death in the family.

Arnie finally found his voice and took control. "If you all have had enough time, I mean if you all are ready, we should be getting on back to the funeral home."

Gladys Jackson lifted a table napkin to her eyes and dabbed away a tear. "We've said our goodbyes. Y'all go ahead and do what you need to do." She looked to her children sitting around her, and they all nodded their agreement.

We just stood there for another painful moment, each of us looking at one another before our eyes drifted downward to the tabletop or the floor. The members of the Jackson family didn't relish having to give up their husband, daddy, and granddaddy, so I understood their not wanting to say much. Arnie and I just wanted to know where we could find the deceased.

The Hospice nurse eventually came to her senses and said, "Oh, I'll see if I can help these gentlemen." She looked at the family. "You all wait in the kitchen. I'll come for you when they're done."

The nurse's name was Glenda. She led us back into the darkness of the hallway, almost to the front screen door, and then she stopped. Her eyes were tired, as if she'd been up most of the night with the Jacksons. "I'll wait for you here."

Arnie and I looked around. To our right the hall opened up into an expansive living room. Two lamps lit opposite corners, but we didn't see the remains of Mr. Jackson. To our left two closed doors hinted that our intended waited for us in the privacy of a bedroom. Arnie looked to Glenda for instruction, but she had pulled out her cell phone to answer a call from another patient's family.

"A or B?" Arnie asked.

I pointed to the one on the right. "A."

Arnie took hold of the worn doorknob and turned. Behind the door, a room stacked floor-to-ceiling with cardboard boxes let us know we'd chosen the wrong door.

"Okay," I said. "B."

Arnie pushed open the door. The bedroom lay still and dim underneath night's cloak. We could make out a tall four-poster bed fashioned out of dark mahogany on the far side of the room between two windows. The scent of peppermint and lavender dominated the room, like what you'd find in one of those crowded tourist shops in Asheville. Several chairs had been pulled up to the bedside, and a marble-top table littered with pill bottles, tissue boxes, and a half empty glass of water testified that the room quartered a sick man. There were overalls hanging on a ladder-back chair, and a pair of slip-on work boots piled the corner. But there was no body.

"What are y'all doing?" Glenda whispered from behind us.

Arnie leaned in close to her. "Looking for Mr. Jackson."

Without a word, Glenda took Arnie by the arm and pulled him out of the room. She directed him toward the front door, pushed open the screen, and stopped on the porch. Arnie looked around. "Okay."

"There he is," Glenda said with a long, pointed finger. "On the swing."

Arnie and I looked at the man on the swing. I walked over to him for a closer look. Sure enough, that was a dead man: eyes open, mouth agape, colorless complexion shaded with gray.

At first I felt like an idiot, but then I remembered that I had been working in the funeral business for only six or seven months, and my ability to distinguish the living from the dead at 3:00 in the morning in hazy light was nowhere close to honed.

"I said 'Hey' to him," Arnie admitted.

"I know," Glenda chuckled. "I was listening from the hall. I wondered why you boys were speaking to a dead man on a swing, but I figured that in your line of work, that might be considered normal."

The Ghosts of Christmas Past

The cold night air felt good against my hot skin after the twenty-five minute hearse ride out to a shallow cove on the lake. With less than a week to go before Christmas, I was looking forward to Christmas Eve dinner at my grandmother's house and a couple of days away from a life consumed by death. Arnie and I had listened to the local radio station's 'round-the-clock "sounds of the season" while we traversed the lonely, dark back roads to make our second house call of the night. It was 2:30 AM, and Santa was "up on the rooftop."

The deputy coroner, a tall man named Ronnie with a dark beard and round spectacles, spotted us across the yard and raised his hand to get our attention.

"I'll go over and talk to Ronnie and find out what's up," Arnie said, and the darkness between the spot where I'd parked the hearse and the old farm house where Ronnie waited with the details of tonight's death consumed the seasoned funeral director.

A couple of EMTs stood behind their ambulance, and I wondered why they were still hanging around. By the time somebody got around to calling the funeral home, their work was pretty much finished. The two men didn't offer so much as a "Hello," so I pulled the cot out of the hearse and waited in the cold.

"Grab some gloves," Arnie instructed when he returned. "Looks like a doozy."

"What do you mean?"

Arnie shook his head. "Just come on."

The deputy coroner met us at the front door of the house, and he held open the screen door as we maneuvered the cot through the narrow opening.

"She's on the sofa," he told us, "on the other side of the room beside the bar."

The room was dark, only a single strand of white Christmas lights shining from the tree in the corner. Arnie reached over and flipped on a reading lamp beside of the sofa, thus adding a meager orange glow to the room. Arnie led the way across the room, and while I could see a body sitting upright on the coach, the details were fuzzy. We approached the body, and I noticed the stale, wood-deep smell of years and years of ciga-rette smoke. The odor permeated every porous surface, and changes in temperature and humidity ensured that the smell never really died.

"Watch your step," Ronnie warned.

Arnie and I both looked down at the cracked linoleum floor and saw a pool of dark blood congealing in the icy night air.

"Is there any way we can get some more light in here?" Arnie asked.

Ronnie walked over to the wall and flipped a switch. The overhead light blazed forth in a sudden, eye-burning bright-ness. Arnie and I blinked a couple of times and then turned our attention to the body for a closer inspection.

Despite the puddle of blood on the floor, everything else in the room appeared fairly neat and orderly. The deceased, a woman who could have been fifty or sixty or seventy years old, appeared to have been a conscientious housekeeper. Arnie released his grip on the cot and stepped closer to the body. I followed him. The deceased sat upright on the couch, her legs crossed at the ankles. She wore faded blue jeans and a pair of fuzzy cloth bedroom shoes. Slung over onto the coffee table were a hard pack of Marlboro Lights and a disposable lighter. A bathroom garbage can rested next to her feet. Her hands were folded across her lap, and she clutched a white linen handkerchief between the fingers of her right hand. Her eyes were open, dull, lifeless orbs staring off into darkness, and her mouth hung slack, like a waterlogged shirt left on the clothesline after a downpour. The television was still on, but the sound was turned down on the Christmas special.

"Look," Arnie said, and he pointed to the handkerchief.

Daubs of blood colored the cotton fabric, and I could see blood spatter on her white sweatshirt. My eyes inched up the dead woman's torso until they rested on her face. Her lips were red, too red for somebody so recently deceased; a dead person usually loses all color when the heart stops beating. Her teeth lay mostly hidden behind her lips, but I could still see that blood had tinted the white enamel a soft pink. Then I noticed a trickle of blood on her chin. A closer inspection of her nose showed more blood, as if both nostrils had suffered a double-barreled nosebleed.

The three of us stood motionless, our minds spinning to make sense of what our eyes saw. To the dead woman's right lay a blood-spattered remote control for the television, and to her left sat an upturned cordless telephone with the antenna pulled halfway out.

"What happened here?"

Ronnie clicked his tongue. "Mrs. Burdette had cancer. She was under Hospice care. The best we can figure is this: She was watching TV by herself. She must have started coughing up blood, and when she couldn't get it to stop, she called 9-1-1. Looks like the coughing must have been bad; she got that trashcan out of the bathroom so she could spit in it, I guess.

She died before the EMTs got here."

"What kind of cancer?" Arnie asked.

"Lung."

I looked back at the cigarettes on the coffee table, a pack of ghosts Mrs. Burdette just couldn't shake, and then down into the flesh-colored garbage can. The bag sagged inside it, and I saw why: It contained enough rich, frothy blood to fill a stewpot. I figured the can could hold over two gallons, and it was half full.

"She bled into the trashcan?" I asked.

Ronnie shook his head. "Apparently so."

"How?"

"My guess is that she threw it up. It came out of her nose and mouth."

I stood amazed. "And the only real mess is this little bit of blood on the floor."

"Yep."

"That has to be over a gallon of blood."

Ronnie shook his head. "That's the way I'd figure it."

Arnie and I leaned in close and studied the bucket of blood. It was deep and dark, and it had a sweet coppery smell. All that blood was inside Mrs. Burdette no more than an hour ago.

Sort of floating in the bucket and sinking at the same time, something solid caught my eye. It was dark and supple, and its ruffled surface reminded me of a wet comforter from a bed. Except for what looked like a sharp, angled tear, its edges were round and smooth.

"What is that?" I asked.

Ronnie looked at Arnie. "Got a pen?"

Arnie fished around in his coat pocket and withdrew a ball-point pen bearing the funeral home name and logo.

Ronnie took the pen and reached into the awful bucket. He stabbed at the piece of tissue until he was able to trap it and slide it slippery and meaty up the inside of the can. It was wrinkled, and a dark, sticky liquid, like tar, streaked the folds. "I'd say is that it's part of her lung."

"Her lung?" Arnie said.

"Yep."

"How did it get … out of her?"

"My guess is that when she started to coughing, she coughed so hard that it tore loose and just came up. According to the Hospice nurse, Mrs. Burdette had smoked all her life. She must have been bent over the trashcan, and that last cough did it."

"She literally coughed up a lung?" I asked.

The deputy coroner looked at Scrooge on the muted television screen and clicked his tongue one last time before turning toward the door. "Yep, she coughed up a lung."

The Embalming Room

She's Alive!

The day I started work at the funeral home, I had attended only three funerals in my life. My great-grandmother, a woman I remember as perpetually grouchy, died when I was six years old, so all I can really recall about her funeral was a church full of people and a white casket. A friend of mine died in a car wreck when I was a junior in high school, and I remember that she looked bloated and uncomfortable in her casket. Her casket was white, and I was a pallbearer. My third funeral experience was the father of a college friend, and for that one, I sat at the back of the church and stayed away from the casket. It wasn't white.

Having not been exposed to the nuances of death enough to build up any sort of tolerance, my first experience in the embalming room with Arnie left me unable to go back to sleep. Nothing remarkable happened that January sometime after midnight, other than the fact that right in front of me lay a dead human body, and an old guy in a green smock worked feverishly to remove all the liquid the body contained and replace it with sharp-smelling embalming fluid that made my eyes water. I felt as though I would pass out twice, but I managed to hang on. Arnie just laughed.

With each new body to embalm, I grew accustomed to working in the preparation room a little more. After six months, I had witnessed just about all there was to see, and rarely did the macabre experience of death get to me by that point. The discomfiting smell of blood, the awkward vulnerability of a deceased loved one whose body must endure the necessary ignominy of the process of embalming, and the unnatural permanence of death's earthly finality: it all got easier. But my full comfort in the presence of death took some time.

When we received the call that a death had just occurred only minutes from the funeral home, Arnie, Clyde Combs, and I were still there finishing up a couple of six-to-eight evening visitations.

"You set up the embalming room," Arnie instructed. "Me and Clyde will make the removal."

No sooner had I laid out the instruments, removed the wooden arm and foot blocks from the cabinet, and added a gallon of water to the embalming machine did Arnie and Clyde return from their mission.

"That was fast," I said, slipping on a pair of latex gloves.

"No family," Clyde explained. "And she lived only two blocks over."

Arnie donned his customary green smock while Clyde and I moved the deceased from the cot to the embalming table.

"I'll clean up the cot and put it back in the hearse," said Clyde as he disappeared behind the closing double doors.

"That's the last we'll see of him tonight," Arnie grunted. "Looks like it's just you and me, kid."

Arnie worked around the body like a man who had been born in an embalming room. While he may have often been awkward around living, breathing humans, Arnie felt most relaxed when he embalmed dead humans. Before I knew it, he had the body positioned and he was already closing the eyes.

"Eye caps," he said.

I passed him two clear bowl-shaped, oval pieces of plastic about the size of the front of a human eye that helped keep the eyelids in place.

"Needle injector."

The pistol-shaped, spring-loaded instrument inserted pointed stainless steel rivets into the skull of the deceased just above the two front teeth and into the deceased's mandible below the middle lower teeth. The sharp popping of metal going into bone resounded through the prep room. Arnie pulled the two pieces of wire tight, closing the deceased's mouth.

"Scissors," he said.

I passed him a pair of six-inch stainless steel blunt-point scissors, and he cut off the stainless injector needle wires protruding from between the deceased's lips

"Mouth former."

I gave him the plastic expression former that he placed between the deceased's teeth and lips.

"Super Glue."

Arnie finished by gluing the deceased's eyes and lips closed, for without working muscles to keep the lids and mouth shut, they were sure to open during visitation; families prefer that this doesn't occur.

Arnie made his incision and located the jugular vein and the carotid artery. With fluid motions, he slipped two twelve-inch pieces of waxed linen thread under the vessels, and before I knew it, he had snipped a small hole in the vein and had inserted the drain tube.

"Pass me the hose."

I lifted the end of the embalming machine hose that held the arterial tube out of its metal holder before unwrapping the eight feet of rubber hose from around the machine. Arne inserted the arterial tube into the carotid artery after using his scissors to cut a small opening.

"Turn it on."

Arnie had already mixed the embalming fluid, so I flipped the small, protruding switch on the front of the Porti-Boy Mark V embalming machine with a three-and-a-half gallon capacity. The familiar sound of the quarter-horse-power motor working up to speed filled the room. I moved back to the head of the embalming table and watched Arnie; my mentor and supervisor simply stood motionless and observed the process.

After about thirty seconds of letting the pressure build, Arnie grasped the drain tube with his left hand and inserted the index finger of his right into the O ring on the end of the plunger and pulled. A gush of deep red, almost maroon blood spewed forth, filling the drain trough on the table's edge.

Almost instantly the deceased's ashen face began to take on the lifelike color of pink as the tinted embalming fluid forced blood out through the jugular vein. Two white towels covering the deceased provided a modicum of modesty, and my eyes fell on the woman's hands folded across her abdomen. Her left hand lay over the right, and Arnie repositioned the wooden block at the deceased's right elbow to allow for better drainage.

When my eyes locked on the dead woman's fingers, I felt a tingle run through my body. I moved closer, my complete focus now on the woman's right thumb. It moved. Her thumb moved! As hesitant at first as a drop of water from a February spigot, her thumb rose slightly and stopped.

I stammered. "Uh, her thumb moved, Arnie."

The words had barely left my mouth when her bent thumb straightened and made a leisurely clockwise sweeping motion. The abductor pollicis brevis, the fat muscle on the outer edge of the palm that controls the thumb, contracted and released, causing the thumb to return to its original position.

"She's alive!" Arnie said, his voice hollow and deep.

Afraid to look away from the dead woman's thumb that had just moved, I shuddered. "Are you serious?"

For months I had heard stories of people declared dead only later to come to life. No, it had never happened to any of the resident embalmers personally, but they'd all heard reports from people who had experienced it. Several news stories had even caught my attention. One was of a woman in Puerto Rico who "died" during child birth only to awaken in the morgue. The other was of a German man who was declared dead and left in the hospital morgue for twenty-four hours; he blinked when the local undertaker unzipped the body bag.

My heart beating fast, I looked back at Arnie. "We need to call 9-1-1 or something!"

Arnie eased onto the bar stool by the wall and grinned. "I can assure you that she's dead."

"But she moved."

"That was just the embalming fluid reacting to her warm muscles. Sometimes it happens." He looked at his watch. "She's been dead, what, less than forty minutes? Her body is still pretty warm, and sometimes when the fluid hits warm muscles, the muscles contract."

I watched the momentarily animate body of Mrs. Thelma Eubanks the rest of the evening, but she failed to capture my wide-eyed attention after her initial terrifying movements. That was okay; I'd seen enough for one night.

You Break It, You Bought It

Stanley Eugene Crutchfield signed on to fight Hitler when he was only seventeen years old. After basic training and months of perfecting his skills at bases in Georgia and Texas, Stanley departed for Europe. He missed D-Day by five months, but there was plenty of fighting left for him when he got to France. He was scheduled to be sent to the Ardennes Region as part of a replacement battalion, but bad weather prevented him from making it past Bastogne, and it was in Bastogne that during a night of heavy shelling by German forces, an artillery shell landed ten feet from where he and several soldiers were running for cover, bounced twice unexploded, and slammed into his right leg. While the shell failed to detonate, the impact shattered his hip. Young Stanley's brief time as a part of World War II was over. He was headed home. That had been nearly sixty-one years earlier.

We took great care in dressing Mr. Crutchfield. He died two days previously after a prolonged battle with pancreatic cancer, and the seventy-nine-year-old's body was frail and withered. Chemotherapy and radiation treatments designed to prolong his life had destroyed all but his spirit; his widow said he remained upbeat and smiling to the last. He died on a Thursday.

Mr. Crutchfield's army uniform had been in storage since his return from battle, and the old fabric had been cut for a younger man. In most cases, veterans' uniforms are too small, but not this time. We tenderly dressed him, building upon him a layered testament to his voluntary service so many years ago. After we put his coat on him, I noticed that Arnie's eyes were red, and I'm sure I saw him wipe away a tear. Even Arnie had a soft spot.

"We need a John," he told me. "We'll add his medals once we place him in the casket."

Without a word, I turned and headed out of the dressing room toward the basement where we parked our pickup hearse and stored everything from wooden caskets to cases of embalming fluid to old files. Lester Polk sat dozing in a chair, his feet propped up on the shoe-shine box, and I asked him to help me get the casket.

"What kind," he asked.

"A John."

He stood and stretched his arms over his head. "'JC and the Boys,'" he said. "We'll have to get one out of the warehouse. None up here."

Lester's seemingly irreverent reference to a 16 gauge steel casket decorated with a depiction of Leonardo di Vinci's *The Last Supper* was little more than a nickname the old timers had used for years. The bronze-tone casket with dark shading was popular, especially with families whose loved ones had spent their lives devoted to God and church.

The heavy casket wasn't on the top row of four, but it was on the third.

"Now who put that thing up there?" Lester asked to no one in particular.

Because of Lester's diminutive stature, getting a casket off the top rack would never happen, and the third row up, while doable, was no place for a heavy 16 gauge; two people could manage it, but only with significant risk of damaging the cas-ket or injuring our backs.

Lester saw Delbert Floyd walking across the parking lot and called for him to help. Lester and Delbert worked on the same shift with another man named Coy Franklin.

"Well, what are y'all doing out here in the dark?" Delbert asked in his usual flippant tone.

"What we're doing," Lester said, "is trying to get this casket from up here where some yo-yo put it."

Delbert looked at the John. "'JC and the Boys.' Y'all know better than to put that casket up that high. It's too heavy. If it fell, somebody could get killed."

He was looking at me.

"I didn't put it up there."

Careful not to let our end of the casket tip down so that the far end lurched up and into the shelf above it, we slid the John almost all the way out. Delbert and I took a side, and maneuvering with strained caution, we lowered it to the waiting casket carriage. Lester held the carriage steady.

Once the casket was secure on the carriage, Delbert turned, grinned, and sauntered out the door. "Merry Christmas," he said with a goofy grin.

"He does know that Christmas is five months away, doesn't he?"

Lester snorted. "Aw, don't pay him no attention. That old fool's been saying that for thirty years."

Lester and I rolled the casket back up to the basement from the warehouse, transferred it to a red velvet-draped casket bier, and made it ready for its new occupant. Once the packing was removed and the outside wiped clean of dust, Lester helped me roll it into the dressing room, the narrow room outside the embalming room.

"We might need your help," Arnie said to Lester, and I could tell that Lester wanted to get back to his nap.

Arnie positioned the casket near the bank of cabinets that held socks, makeup, and an array of plastic undergarments designed to prevent unwanted leakage. The casket was a half-couch sealer. The "half couch" part meant that in order to put a body inside, two separate sections had to be opened for full access; "sealer" meant that once the casket was closed prior to interment, a rubber gasket around the opening helped to create an airtight, watertight seal.

"We won't need the lift," Arnie informed us, referring to the device whose hydraulics enabled us to lift and casket bodies too heavy for us to handle on our own.

The three of us lined up parallel to the body and prepared to lift: Arnie on the head, Lester at the feet, and me stuck in the middle as usual. Arnie made sure the deceased's head was secure and wouldn't flop backward and cause the mouth to pop open. I wiggled one of my arms under the lower half of the torso and the other under the hips. Lester took command of the feet.

"Easy does it," cautioned Arnie.

We raised Mr. Crutchfield's earthly remains with all the gentleness one would employ to pick up a sleeping baby from a crib. But that didn't mean it was easy. From the outset, I knew that being in the middle, I bore the brunt of the load. As soon as we stood upright and began to sidestep toward the waiting casket, the dressing room door opened and in walked the owner of the funeral home.

Conveying the true nature of some funeral home owners can be challenging. Some owners, especially those with small funeral homes, make sure they are involved in all aspects of the business. Nothing happens – no dime spent, no body prepared, no family served, no spade of dirt turned – that they don't know about. Other owners rarely darken the doorways of their establishments, content to allow the hired help to generate revenue for them. Our boss fell somewhere in the middle, and we liked it that way. He kept office hours on weekdays, and he strove to make an appearance on as many funerals as he could manage with his busy social schedule. That said, rarely did he dictate how we were to handle the day-to-day operations of the funeral home. In fact, he seldom visited the more intimate venues in the funeral home, and the dressing room was one of those areas.

"Who do we have here, Arnie?" he asked, his voice full and bright.

"Mr. Crutchfield," Arnie grunted.

"Looks like he was in the military."

Arnie shook his head, his eyes rolling slightly upward. "World War II. France."

We stopped halfway to the casket, for our employer had moved closer to us and stood blocking our way. While Mr. Crutchfield wasn't terribly heavy, the longer I stood there without moving, the more I began to feel the strain. The boss examined the veteran's uniform, pausing to ask Arnie questions about this or that symbol.

"Well, why don't you all go ahead and place Mr. Crutchfield inside his casket," he finally suggested.

I could tell that Arnie wanted to say something like, *we would if you would get out of our way*; instead, he grinned and said, "Good idea, sir."

My shoulders burned as we lined up with the casket and began to lower the body onto the waiting bed. Most old timers agreed that we had only one shot at positioning the body just right, so Arnie slowed us down in order to get the head and shoulders in the right spot.

"Okay," he said.

The burning in my shoulders moved to my back, and I lowered the body a little too fast. Lester had already let go of the feet, and he slumped against the back wall to catch his breath. When I felt the full weight of the body settle atop the fabric interior, I knew we were good. Before I could pull out my arms and back away, though, I heard an unexpected creak of metal as the foot end of the casket fell closed, slamming hard onto my back. I let out a little yelp when a pointed piece of metal – the one jutting out from the cap that fits into a hole on the lower part of the casket to help create the seal – dug into my back.

All of a sudden everything was dark. Time seemed to stand still as I came to grasp with the fact that my arms were wedged underneath a dead body with the closed casket cap preventing me from freeing myself.

"My goodness," the boss said, and I thought I could hear the genuine concern in his voice. "Get him out of there."

Lester hustled over and raised the casket lid while Arnie helped me extract my arms without messing up Mr. Crutchfield's uniform.

"Be careful," the owner of the funeral home said as he pushed past me, and for a split second I was touched by his sincerity. "Be careful that you don't damage this casket."

He fussed around the casket, inspecting Jesus and the disciples and every corner and hinge. "These caskets are expensive," he said, and then he turned to me. "You're going to have to pay more attention to what you're doing around here."

"Yes, sir," I said as I rubbed the knot on my back. "I'll do that."

With his long fingers massaging his temples, he backed out of the dressing room and disappeared down the hallway.

Lester put his hand on my shoulder. "You all right?"

"I think so."

Arnie laughed. "You know the old saying: 'You break it, you bought it'."

Running Out of Time

The dead man needed the mold cleaned off his face.

"You can take care of it," Arnie told me. "Lord knows the rest of us have done it enough."

I grabbed a bottle of strong-smelling Dry Wash off the shelf above the embalming machine and walked back out to the dressing room.

"Wrap some of that cotton gauze around a pair of hemo-stats," Arnie said over his shoulder. He was in the middle of removing Mrs. Delfino's viscera from the red plastic bag that had been deposited inside her abdominal cavity after her autopsy. Once he got her heart, liver, both lungs, kidneys, stomach, and whatever else was inside the bag out, he would treat it all with embalming fluid and place the organs back inside Mrs. Delfino. "Dip the cotton in the Dry Wash and wipe his face, neck, and hands gently; and don't get anything on his clothes, especially his shirt collar."

Mr. Winkle had died over six months ago, and since then, he had become a permanent fixture in our dressing room.

"And tell me again why is Mr. Winkle still here?"

"Don't know for sure," Arnie said from the other room.

"Best I understand it, nobody's claimed him yet."

"I thought the City got involved and we buried the ones without any family to Potters' Field." The green mold was so thick on Mr. Winkle's neck that I had to scrub harder. I was afraid I would break his skin.

"That's right."

"Then why haven't we taken Mr. Winkle out to Potters' Field?"

"Mr. Winkle is apparently the cousin or nephew or step-brother twice removed of somebody well-known. They're still trying to figure out who the next of kin is. It's been in the courts for months now, and we can't do anything with him until somebody decides."

"But six months?"

"There's apparently a wife and an ex-wife and a girlfriend involved. A couple of biological children seem to be fighting several step-children who have been challenged by some illegitimates popping up from the underside of this and that rock."

"Well, if he's got a wife, shouldn't she be in charge?" I asked.

"I believe so, but they were apparently in the process of getting divorced. He had a little money from his famous relative, so now everybody wants a piece of the pie."

After I cleaned the mold off Mr. Winkle's face, neck, and hands, I dampened a clean towel with some tap water and gave his skin a good wiping.

"Now redo his make-up," Arnie said. I noticed that he was struggling with what looked like intestines. Based on the strong twang coming from the embalming room, I'd say he'd punctured them.

Before I started reapplying a fresh coat of cosmetics to Mr. Winkle's ashen face and hands, I used the whisk broom to knock off the thin layer of dust (mostly baby powder and face powder) from his clothes. I checked the label on the suit: Hartz, Shafer, and Marks. Both the slacks and the coat had seen better days, but twenty years earlier, they would have been the finest money could have bought, at least in our neck of the woods.

The skin on Mr. Winkle's cheeks and beneath his eyes had started to sag. Arnie had already told me once that if we didn't hurry up and do something with him, the man's skin would start to fall off.

"Like a snake shucking its outer layer," Arnie'd said without so much as a chuckle.

I knew that Arnie had already re-injected Mr. Winkle with embalming fluid a half dozen times. I wondered how much a body could take before embalming fluid started eating through muscle, tissue, and skin and come oozing out like Coke through the bottom of yesterday's paper McDonald's cup.

After I added some color to his face and hands, I stood back and studied Mr. Winkle. He look like he always had, lying there perfectly content on that white porcelain dressing table waiting for the assorted legal, illegal, current, previous, and wannabe Winkles to settle their differences. I noticed that his stomach, never really what anyone would call flat, protruded more than usual.

"Arnie, he might need to let off a little gas," I said.

This time Arnie turned around so he could assess the swelling for himself. The front of his smock was covered in so much blood that he looked like a slaughterhouse butcher. Embalming a body that had endured the ravages of a post-mortem examination was never any fun, but I could tell that Arnie was having a tough time with this one. "Yep, he's bloated, all right. You know what to do."

Yes, I knew what to do, but that didn't mean I wanted to do it. I unbuttoned Mr. Winkle's coat and laid the two matching sections of the front of the coat off to each side. With nimble fingers, I undid each button on his white shirt, and after pushing it to the side, I lifted the white t-shirt. On the left side of the stomach, about one inch above the belly button and two inches to the left, the plastic trocar button waited to be removed. Using the trocar button applicator, I worked the flesh-colored button counterclockwise until it popped out with a swoosh of air.

"Wow," I said more to myself than anyone else.

"Oh, my, that's bad," Arnie said from the preparation room. "And if I can smell it in here, I can only imagine what it smells like in there. Press down on the abdomen a little and get some more gas out, and then put that button back in."

Once Mr. Winkle's midsection was more or less flat again, I replaced the trocar button. With his undershirt smoothed, his shirt buttoned and retucked, and his slacks and belt back to normal, I buttoned his jacket and reviewed my handwork.

"Looks pretty good to me," I said.

Arnie, ever critical, ever the teacher, stood behind me and surveyed my handiwork. "Not bad," he said. "You could have probably gotten a little more gas out, and his make-up looks a little heavier on his right side; other than that, I'll give you an A-."

"Thanks."

"You're getting there," he said. "We might make an embalmer out of you yet." Arnie turned and stepped back to his autopsied body. "Go ahead and put a new white sheet on Mr. Winkle and roll him back over to the corner. You did such a good job on him, go ahead and plan to do it all again in another week to ten days."

"What if he's gone by then?"

Arnie chuckled from behind his plastic face shield. "I wouldn't worry too much about it," he said. "I'm sure he'll still be around."

Arnie was right, but only by a couple of days. With no family and no friends in attendance, we buried Ronald Winkle in corner plot at the City cemetery. He'd been on this earth sixty-three years; nearly six months of it though, he spent as a guest of our dressing room.

Goin' Home

When Coy Franklin told me to grab an isolation suit and for me to follow him down to the garage at the end of the parking lot, I had a pretty good idea what was coming. Back then there were times that we kept long-dead bodies, overexposed corpses far beyond mere human repair, secured away from the main building. These cadavers reposed more efficiently in isolation, lingering behind the squeaky roll-up door in the distant building. Based on past experience, this location was the most suitable should a rapidly decomposing body begin to leak; any unwelcome drips could be washed down the floor drain quick as a whip.

It was cold and rainy that afternoon as we made the short walk to the expansive garage where the funeral home's limousines, hearses, vans, and sedans waited for the next opportunity to be of service. Directly in front of us, the shut bay door prevented curious sightseers from getting a glimpse of the chipped porcelain table at the very back of the cement basin, a wrinkled white sheet draped over it and hanging so that only its forty-year old, nibbled-down wheels stuck out. Passersby would have little clue as to what waited beneath the sheet; we, on the other hand, knew exactly what we were in for.

A cocksure Delbert Floyd sauntered ahead and entered first via the rear walk-through door. As we approached from the outside and waited, he raised the outer door with a groan and bade us enter. At first, the smell was mild, easier on the nose that what we were used to. I was awful glad and wondered if our task might prove more pleasant than we expected.

Funeral directors are frequently called upon to undertake the most unpleasant of tasks, tasks that accountants, teachers, lawyers, and the sales staff at the local department store

 D.S. Bradley

might find objectionable. And while this darker variety of life's necessities remains unpleasant to this day, somebody has to do it. Human bodies do decompose beyond the possibility of the temporary preservation that embalming affords; nonetheless, families still need the closure that comes with a final viewing or a visitation or a funeral service. Heartbroken family members need to know that the casket will be lowered into the grave, and upon their return to the cemetery, a peaceful spot above-ground, complete with a temporary bench, has been reserved for the next phase of the grieving process. Grass will grow, and the broken earth will heal right along with those left to mourn the loss, and the funeral directors, to the best of their terrestrial abilities and within the constraints of what nature presents them, make it all happen.

So it was that a crew of four men finally gathered inside the dank room before the door fell closed behind us. The deceased's new casket, which Arnie Maddox and Lester Polk had brought along with them as they made their way down the hill, bided its time.

"Well," Coy asked, "y'all want to set him down on the floor so we can put the lime in the pouch?"

The "pouch" to which Coy referred was actually a thick, black body bag from the county morgue, and that meant one of us would have to unzip the zipper and spread open the sides; somebody would then add lime and embalming powder.

Nobody really felt much like saying anything at that point. Pouring off-white, powdery lime around an eight-day-dead body tends to conjure up images most people find difficult to digest, and funeral directors, while content to perform their duty, are no different. Working with death is one thing; working with week-old death without the benefit of embalming is another matter entirely.

"Let's go ahead," I said.

The deceased was lighter than we expected. Using the straps on the sides of the bag, four of us gently, carefully lowered the body bag to a sheet on the cement floor. This sudden movement after a commotion-free week of repose stirred up the smell. Ah, yes. That was it, the unmistakable odor of a rotting person. There's no other stink like it. No dead animal in the world smells like a long-dead body. Arnie told me early on in my funeral career that the human body smelled so bad because of all the chemicals in our diet, and I was beginning to think he may have been on to something. And once that smell gets into your hair and clothes, it stays with you a few days to remind you to appreciate life a little bit more.

"Go ahead and open the pouch," Coy instructed. "He ain't gonna get himself ready."

Delbert, who'd been working at the funeral home for over twenty years, jumped in, always eager to get the job done. I watched from a safe distance should anything unexpected spring forth from the darkness. Evidence of an unidentified dried liquid smeared across the top of the pouch warned me that there could be anything gooey or gross or just plain dangerous within a hand's reach. I was glad I had on gloves, the good ones that came individually wrapped by the pair.

"Oops," Delbert whispered. The zipper ripped right there in his hands, leaving the bag's contents partially exposed. He looked up with eyebrows raised. "That's not good."

"Go ahead an open it on up best you can," Coy said. "We still got work to do here." He took a drag from his unfiltered Camel before flicking it toward the slender crack between the garage door and the floor. "Somebody run back up to the basement and grab another bag."

Delbert pulled back suddenly in retreat and stood. "I'll be right back. Y'all don't go anywhere without me."

Arnie, swaddled from head to toe in his white isolation suit and looking a little too much like a deflated marshmallow, slipped up close and poured a one-pound bag of lime in the disabled body bag. That was the first real opportunity to view the deceased. Wide swaths of skin and tissue had already slipped clean of the muscle, and the muscle was the color of boiled meat. The eyelids had recessed, leaving sunken orbitals staring at nothing; the man's mouth had fallen open in silent release.

By this point we had all pretty much gotten used to the smell. But it wasn't so much the rotten fetor stinging our noses and saturating our clothing as much as the realization that any one of us could, with enough time to properly stew, emit the same genuinely disgusting funk. What we had before us was a dead body that had begun to rot where it fell at the deceased's home. A passing relative had discovered the body slumped over in a corner on the back porch, shoe-horned in between the Kenmore washer and the wall. The coroner estimated the body to have been there about six days. Once he finished his investigation, the resident experts at the funeral home ascertained that any attempt to embalm the body would be an exercise in futility. So the body, enclosed in the black body bag, lying atop the old porcelain table, and draped with a white pall, had been wheeled into the wash bay to await further preparation. The cold air of late autumn would retard continued decomposition while funeral day approached.

And now it was funeral day, the day every family dreads while at the same time knowing it will occur again and again and again if we live long enough. Funeral day was what had called us all to gather 'round the deceased to ready the body for the final leg of the journey. In just a couple of hours, family and friends would assemble in a peaceful stateroom to celebrate another life that reached its inevitable end. But this service would be different. There would be no body to view, no body lying in repose as mourners shuffled past with glistening eyes.

A casket would be there, though, a fitting reminder for us all that death awaits. That locked and sealed casket, with a lime buffer, would protect the heart-broken family from intolerable death and the smell that always comes with it.

As we lifted the original body bag so that we could seal it inside a fresh bag, the stench escaped its hibernation, gassing us, exposing us to the worst death had to offer. Someone quickly, I can't remember who it was, for I may have momentarily swooned in the wake of the olfactory onslaught, poured in a bottle of acrid-smelling embalming powder and a little more lime. Delbert, perhaps sensing some responsibility for having ripped the original bag in the first place, had returned, and he immediately zipped the outer bag with an audible sigh of relief. The odor, however, remained. But why not? Trapped there inside the warm wash bay, where was the offensive tang to go? I looked down at the casket on the floor beside us, and I motioned for my colleagues to step forth.

Once we had the two bags safely inside the dark blue casket complete with embroidered doves in heavenward flight on the inner cap, a casket we affectionately referred to as the "Goin' Home," Coy resumed command and moved forward with a glass bottle of glue and a small wand. He brushed the thick, gel-like liquid over the length of the outer zipper.

"Whew," Arnie said, wiping the sting from his eyes. "I think I like smell of that glue better."

For once, we all welcomed the strong scent of the glue. Intoxicating and probably carcinogenic as it was, I lifted my white mask for a fresh whiff of glue-corrupted air. What I smelled may as well have been gardenias or roses, for by any other name, it would still have smelled so much sweeter.

We hoisted the casket back to the bier, wiped away any dust from its polished surface, and raised the garage door to a burst of refreshing cold air.

"You run along and get the casket spray ready," Coy told me, and he patted the casket, his expression paternal. "Sometimes our work ain't pretty, but it's got to be done." He shooed me on out the door. "Hurry up, now. This boy's got a funeral to go to. He's goin' home."

The Visitation (or Layin' a Corpse)

Come and Get It, Boys!

I've heard that the term funeral home gets its name from the fact that at one time the only place that provided enough room for a body to repose was back at the family home. A precursor to funeral home was funeral parlor. A parlor is a place where we sit around and talk and welcome guests into our homes. Parlors today have become places for television and video games, but their origins are much more genteel.

Part of the funeral ritual is the receiving of guests. For some folks, it's called "receiving friends," while others call it a wake. Whichever term you prefer, most families desire a place of comfort where they can mourn the loss of a beloved family member in decorative style while still having plenty of room to sit around and talk. When houses ceased to have grand parlors that could accommodate Grandma's knitting circle, the WMU, her Sunday school class, her still ambulatory friends from high school, and the bunch who met every morning at Hardee's for sausage biscuits and coffee (not to mention all her relatives), funeral homes took up the slack.

These spacious buildings of comfortable staterooms provide all the coziness of home with none of the mess-up or clean-up. Some people, though, still remember with fondness when Uncle Joe died and the morticians hauled his remains back to the house and set his casket up on two straight-back chairs in the parlor in front of the big window next to the fire place. To hear them tell it, they didn't even have electricity back then. It was like something out of Mark Twain's *Huckleberry Finn*. And the people. Why, people came from all over to pay their last respects; on top of that, it was good to have Uncle Joe back home one last time.

Even today people do request that the funeral directors take their loved ones back home for one last visit. Arnie and I had been off the weekend, and when I came downstairs that Monday morning after sitting at the receptionist's desk on the main viewing floor long enough for the receptionist to repair an unsightly run in her hose, he told me to put my coat back on and follow him.

"We need to go out to a house and check some makeup," he said as he slipped behind the wheel of the company station wagon. "They took a body home yesterday, and there's a good chance it needs to be touched up this morning."

If people years ago took bodies home because they had the room, it seems that people today take bodies home for exactly the opposite reason: the smaller the house, the more likely they are to take Mama home. The house we pulled up to sat on a lonely stretch of road heading out of town in the direction of Georgia. From the driveway, the house looked like it couldn't be more than a five or six rooms at best, and that was counting at least two additions, one on the side and another on the front.

The eight steps ascending to the front porch were crooked, and I wondered when the whole thing might topple over and flatten us. From top step to front door couldn't have been more than four feet, and the doorway was dark and narrow.

"How'd they get the casket in here?" I whispered when I thought about a casket a good six and half feet long and close to three feet wide.

"Probably took it through a back door," Arnie said.

He knocked on the door, and soon a little bulldog of a man popped out of the shadows.

"Yeah?"

"I'm Arnie Maddox," he said, and then he turned toward me, "and this is uh, um … Anyway, we're from the funeral home."

The man looked at us through the dirty screen. In his right hand he held a crusty brown cup, into which he spat slowly, and in his other he held the grimy remote control for the television. "I'm Junior. I told that man that waited on us that I wouldn't have the rest of the money for Daddy's funeral service before the end of the week."

"That's fine," Arnie said. "We're not here for that. We're here to check your daddy's make up. We need to see if it needs fixing."

Satisfied that we weren't bill collecting, Junior admitted us. The furniture had seen better days, but everything appeared clean and in good order. Two hounds of muddled background lounged by a rear door, and I could see that Arnie was probably right about the casket having come in that way.

Junior watched as Arnie repaired the places where people had rubbed the dead man's hands and kissed his face. "Don't make him up too much," he said. "I don't reckon my daddy would be too happy if he knew somebody was rouging up his cheeks."

"We'll keep it light," said Arnie.

I heard some commotion in the back room, and presently a tall boy of about sixteen or seventeen strolled out clad only in his boxer shorts. He looked over at us before snorting and collapsing into a worn out recliner.

"That's my boy, Alan" Junior said. "He ain't taking the passing of his granddaddy real good."

I looked over at Alan. He had his head thrown back across the arm of the chair, his mouth wide open so that he put me in mind of the dead man.

"I don't see why y'all got to put make up on him," Alan complained. "He looked just fine without it."

Arnie put the cap on the makeup bottle and turned to face Alan. "Young man," Arnie began. "The one thing that gives a body its constant color and perkiness is blood pressure. Blood pressure keeps your lips and cheeks full. Your grandfather doesn't have a blood pressure, and he needs this make up so he doesn't look gray. It's just part of what we do."

That seemed to satisfy the boy, for he threw his head back again and started hocking up something from way back in his throat.

When Arnie finished his repair job, the body lying in the casket looked as peaceful as a man taking an afternoon nap. No one would have thought that forty years working in the cotton mill had filled his lungs and veins and heart with enough lint to make a bed sheet. That and smoking a couple packs a day had finally done him in.

Arnie was packing up a little black bag with his assortment of makeup bottles when somebody knocked on the door.

"Come on in, Preacher," Junior said. He turned toward his son. "Alan, get up and get some clothes on. The preacher's here."

Alan wrestled a second or two longer with whatever foul bit he'd resurrected from the back of his throat before heeding his daddy's word and slugging off to the bedroom. I could tell that boy was going to one more handful pretty soon, if he wasn't already.

"Junior, I brung you some fried chicken," the preacher said. "It's from the Bi-Lo over on the Bypass."

Junior took the navy blue box and held it up high. He then pulled it down to eye level and peered over the side at thighs, wings, legs, and breasts. "Thank you, Preacher. That smells mighty good."

He was right about the smell. I ate a fairly big breakfast, but the smell of that chicken woke up my stomach early for lunch. I noticed that Arnie was staring at the box, too, and I saw his fingers reach around an imaginary chicken leg.

"Glad to do it, Junior. I knew y'all might need something for lunch, so I picked it up on the way."

"Yes, sir," continued Junior. "We sure do appreciate this."

From the preacher's first steps into the room, the two hounds lingering by the back door moved to attention. They had their noses pointed up in the air as if they were sniffing out a 'coon. Their tails beat hard against the wooden floor, and the big brown one started to salivate. As soon as Junior lowered the box to peer inside, both dogs stood up and locked their master in a tight gaze. They wanted to pant, but they kept their mouths closed and their eyes fixed on that chicken.

Outside the back door I heard a commotion. More dogs scratched and whined; they must have either smelled the fried chicken or sensed the excitement of the other dogs. I saw a couple of floppy-eared heads bounce in and out of sight in the window frame.

"Come on now," Junior said, and we all knew he wasn't talking to us.

He walked over toward the two dogs on this side of the back door, and the dogs started bouncing and grunting with the delight that is born of anticipation. Junior pushed his way between the hounds and opened the back door. Quicker than lightning, the two dogs raced outside, knocking four or five other big dogs out of the way.

"Here now!" called out Junior. "Let's go, boys!"

A chorus of barking, moaning, and whining rose up from the pack of dogs. They zipped and weaved around the porch like flies on roadkill, their long toenails clicking against the paintless wooden floor. Junior stood there watching them, taunting them for a good minute or more before he finally spoke.

"Come and get it, boys!" he shouted as he pulled a fat, grease-dripping breast from the box. "We got us some fried chicken!"

He tossed that breast into the air, and seven mouths, tongues draped over their blue lips like Sunday coats hanging over kitchen chairs, snapped in unison. Before the breast began its descent into some dog's waiting gullet, Junior was already chucking out a thigh. As five or six snarling, growling dogs began to fight over those chicken pieces, Junior grasped two legs antennae-like in his fist and shot them a little farther out into the yard. Next came another breast. A couple of a wings. Three more thighs. Another leg.

By now slack-jawed Alan had returned outfitted in a pair of dirty Wranglers and a t-shirt that read "Don't make me do it." He stopped at the middle of the room and watched his daddy.

I looked over to the Pentecostal Holiness preacher, and he hadn't moved, but his eyes were all scrunched up under bushy brown brows, and I wondered what in the world that man was thinking. Here he was bringing good fried chicken to this grieving family, and the dead man's son was feeding it to the yard dogs. The grin spreading across Arnie's red face told me that this was something new the veteran embalmer had yet to witness in all his years as a funeral director.

"What you doing throwing out all the chicken?" Alan asked, and I thought that was the first sensible words to cross the boy's lips yet.

Junior threw out a final chicken breast to the dogs that had quieted considerably in direct proportion to the sharp-edged chicken bones already making their jagged way toward intestines any veterinarian would agree weren't suited for poultry. "Aw, hush up, now," Junior answered, and he turned the box over, the crumbs falling like rain on the dogs' heads. "This is just cheap ol' grocery-store chicken." He slammed the door and dropped the box onto the floor by a bulging black garbage bag. "Your mama's church class is bringing over the good stuff from Kentucky Fried Chicken in about an hour."

Revelations

Clyde Combs grinned and gave a half-hearted salute as his tall, gangly frame disappeared behind the closing double doors that led to the back hallway from the main floor of the funeral home.

Arnie Maddox looked at his watch. "Nine o'clock," he said.

We both knew what that meant. On our shift, each man took a turn remaining on the viewing floor after nine o'clock. Most visitations back then ran from 7:00 – 9:00 PM, and when the families still hadn't left at nine o'clock, the two men not staying to close up the building left. It was my night to stay, so Arnie drove to his house about fifteen minutes away, and Clyde went upstairs to watch television in the apartment on the top floor.

"Call me," Arnie instructed. As the senior man and the embalmer on our shift, he was our supervisor.

Before he could walk away, several people appeared in the wide hallway from what we called the James Street Room at the back of the building. Arnie and I walked over and spoke to the remaining members of the Brown family. Yes, they were tired. No, they didn't need anything. Yes, they would see us tomorrow.

We escorted them to the back door, wished them a good night's rest, and walked back to the desk.

"One down, one to go," Arnie said as he turned to leave. "Maybe the people up front won't take too long."

After I watched Arnie step behind the same door where Clyde had vanished fifteen minutes earlier, I turned my attention to the stateroom at the front of the hall. Our funeral home had seven such rooms to accommodate seven families at any given time. If necessary, we could also use our chapel. I had worked nights when bodies lay in repose in all seven rooms, but I had yet to endure seven official visitations.

Visitations usually took on a life of their own. Some of the employees who worked visitations enjoyed their time standing around for two or three hours while hordes of people laughed a little too much and talked a little too loudly. Visitation was a time to speak to old friends, greet visitors, and play host and hostess. I learned early on in my time as a funeral man, however, that visitations bored me. I didn't like all the standing around, helping people find their desired mourning family, pointing out the restrooms, or fetching cups of water.

That particular night I was not in the best of moods. I had arrived at work at eight o'clock that morning, and then I spent the whole day working a couple of funerals. On both services I drove the hearse, which meant before the services I had to stand out in the heat and park cars, and after the committals I had to stay late and cover the graves. By the time I got back in after the second service, it was nearly six o'clock and people were already gathering for the two visitations. Arnie had mercy on me and told me to take thirty minutes downstairs: wash up, get a Coke and a pack of crackers, and sit down for a few minutes. That felt like a lifetime ago.

The Varner family had been assigned the Presbyterian Room, the first room on the left just inside the front door. Arnie said it had always been called the Presbyterian Room, most likely because the owners of the funeral home were Presbyterians. Across the hall was the Gardenside Room; a small prayer garden was located outside that room. We were also proud to offer the O'Donnell Room, the Middle Room, the Harold White Room, the Corner Room, and the James Street Room.

About half the time, the families assigned to the Presbyterian Room turned out to be friends of the owners or fellow church members, and that meant that we usually treated those families, not differently, but with softer kid gloves. Neither Arnie, Clyde, nor I helped families make funeral arrangements, so we often found ourselves in the dark when it came to the mysterious reason this or that family was assigned one of the smaller, yet more prestigious, rooms in the building.

At 9:30, people began to gather in the hallway outside the Presbyterian Room. I walked up to the front of the hall, offered my best supportive smile, and asked if everything was okay. The person in charge, a tall, slender woman who wore a little black dress and her blonde hair pulled back into a pony tail, assured me that despite the modest turnout, everything was fine. After several awkward minutes of small talk, the attractive woman took the family matriarch by the arm, and the two of them led the family out onto the porch. Grinning at my good fortune, I followed the group outside, said goodbye, and watched as seven little black dresses, five navy sport coats over khaki pants, a handful of children, and a couple of slow aunts and uncles walked across the dark parking lot to their waiting SUVs and Buicks. Time to close shop.

Loosening my tie as I walked back through the front door, I almost began to sing. Several months earlier I had started singing each night as I turned off the lights, a habit Arnie attributed to his belief that I was afraid to be in the funeral home alone after dark. Before I could produce even the first note, unexpected voices stopped me. I had just locked the front door when I heard people talking. I peered down the hallway, but the wide expanse that was earlier filled with people now stood empty. As I straightened my tie, I looked around the corner into the Presbyterian Room, and there sat two men in their middle thirties stretched out and comfortable on the antique sofa. One man looked at me, but when I did not speak, he returned his attention to the other man's story. Crestfallen, I finished tightening the knot on my necktie and made my way back to the desk. It was 9:41.

Because the old timers at the funeral home drilled into our heads that we never, never rushed a family, I sat quietly at the desk with the full weight of my silent burden bearing down upon me. Yes, I wanted lock up and douse the lights. Yes, I was tired and ready to lose myself under the cool white sheets in the bed that awaited my arrival in the upstairs apartment. No, I would never willingly rush a grieving family or make them feel uncomfortable.

We were always telling families to take their time.

"This concludes the committal service," Coy Franklin and Hoke Harris, the two funeral directors who directed all the funerals, liked to say to the family who sat beneath the tent at the cemetery. "Y'all take all the time you need. We're in no hurry." And Coy or Hoke would grin, pat me on the back, and drive off in the lead car, leaving me to wait out the family and then close the grave.

"Y'all stay as long as you like," the owner would tell a family when he met them at the beginning of a visitation. "These boys," and he looked back at Arnie, Clyde, and me, "will be here all night if necessary." All we could do was smile and nod our heads as the owner patted each of us on the back and went home to dinner.

"I'm going to close these doors," Delbert Floyd was fond of saying when he went in to assist a family for their first viewing of their deceased loved one. "You all just take your time. We'll be right outside waiting." And wait we would. I've waited hours for families to wrap up their first viewing.

Even Arnie, who spent most of his time locked in the windowless embalming room, couldn't break free of twenty years of "take your time" indoctrination. "I'll be right outside this door," he told family members who, for whatever reason, needed to view the deceased in our preparation room instead of waiting until the body had been embalmed, washed, dressed, cosmetized, and casketed. "Y'all take as much time as you need. We're not in any hurry."

I think our motto should have been "Hurry up and wait."

At ten o'clock, one hour after the visitation officially concluded, I stood from the desk, buttoned the top button of my charcoal suit coat, and slowly strode up the hall toward the front door. Before I reached the middle of the hallway, I heard their voices. Laughter erupted as the two men came into view, and this time both of them looked my way. I smiled, nodded, and walked through the front door and out onto the porch. The smell of cigarettes lingered in the ashtrays. I watched the traffic moving along Main Street, and when I felt my demeanor calming enough to do my job, I stepped back inside.

With the two men reclining on the sofa and enjoying their conversation, I ambled through the state rooms, peering into drawers of old dressers and opening antique pie safes to see what I could find. When I finally made my way back around to the desk, the big grandfather clock was just striking the half hour – it was 10:30.

I thought of Clyde; he had probably fallen asleep on the couch in the den watching television. Arnie would already be in bed; he had worked in the funeral business enough years to know that an embalmer got some sleep with the living, for the dead would be calling out his name in the quiet hours of the morning soon enough.

For the next thirty minutes I read the two local papers cover-to-cover. Both contained the same old, same old, except for the fact that the obituary pages in each had been torn out, leaving a jagged scar as a reminder of where they once had been. Downstairs in a small closet, piles and piles of obituary pages through the years waited for disposal after the area deaths had been cataloged by a pale secretary in a corner office.

Eleven o'clock. I felt my face getting flush with indignation. How dare these people stay so long? I knew I shouldn't get angry, but these people were sitting up there talking while I could be sleeping. They could talk at home. But they were family members. Their dead grandfather or great uncle lay in quiet repose twelve feet away; and besides, we never rushed family members. In an act of defiance, I removed by suit coat and hung it over the back of the chair. Once again I headed toward the front, and this time I rolled up my shirt sleeves while I walked. And there they sat. Neither appeared to have moved, and neither paid me any attention this time.

I peered out the front door – same old traffic, same stale cigarette smell. I turned out the lights in the Gardenside Room, the Middle Room, and the O'Donnell Room. Then I stepped across the hall and used the breaker box to extinguish all the lights in the back half of the building. Maybe this will get their attention, I thought. And wouldn't you know it: Neither one of those fellows so much as stepped a toe outside that room for the next hour.

The old clock's marking the beginning of the witching hour jerked me from my sleep. Getting my bearings took some time, and for a second or two I didn't know where I was. My elbows ached from where I'd fallen asleep with my head in my hands at the desk. I stood and stretched, the reality that I was stuck in a visitation nightmare suddenly becoming a reality. With a sigh, I pointed my feet toward the Presbyterian Room. Sleep had calmed my irritation at the gall of these people to sit up talking until midnight when I needed to go to bed, but the resolution that replaced it might prove more dangerous.

"Gentleman," I said when I stepped into the room.

The men ceased their conversation, and two sets of eyes found mine. My first inclination was to simply tell them to go home. I wanted to kick them out into the warm night and turn out the porch light while they lingered beneath it, but my devotion to my responsibilities prevented such defiance.

Instead, I reverted back to my training, back to the manners my parents and grandparents had instilled so thoroughly in me. "I just wanted to check," I said with a sigh, "to see if you needed anything."

Revelations usually pop up at the most unexpected times. By their very nature, revelations bring to light unforeseen conclusions or information that might have proved useful earlier on. F. Scott Fitzgerald's Nick Carraway put it best when he spoke of an "intimate revelation...quivering on the horizon." I knew that a revelation hung just above our heads when I observed the expression on the man's face as he started to speak.

"Oh, we're not part of the family," he admitted.

The other man completed the revelation. "We're just two college friends catching up on the old days. We're from out of town and aren't staying for the funeral tomorrow."

The first man laughed. "We were wondering when you would tell us to leave."

"It's time for you to leave," I said, my words devoid of any emotion.

I turned and stepped over to the front door. Holding it open, I ushered the two college buddies out into the muggy night. Before any one of us could utter a syllable, I pulled the door closed, turned the two locks, and switched off the porch light while the two men lingered beneath it.

With what little energy I had left, I climbed the stairs to the apartment. I brushed my teeth and hung my clothes in the narrow closet. Never could I remember a bed more inviting than the one before me. Exhausted, yet surprisingly giddy, I slipped beneath the cool white sheets, my head sinking into the fresh pillow. Almost instantly, my thoughts fell into a pattern of random and bizarre. Like a welcome revelation, sleep quivered on the horizon just long enough for me to appreciate its approach.

Sometime later the telephone rang. It could have been five seconds, five minutes, or five hours: it didn't matter. That awful, sudden, disquieting, hateful sound jerked me from my sleep; my heart pounded so that I could feel it in my toes and my temples.

"Funeral home," I answered through the fog.

"This is Nancy at the hospital. We have a family requesting your services."

The Funeral Service

The Run-Around

The casket was so heavy that the wheels beneath the red, velvet-draped bier carrying it mired up in the carpet.

"You gonna have to pull on that end and help me with this thing," whispered Lester Polk.

Lester had worked at the funeral home since before my mama and daddy got married back in 1964. He started when he was a teenager and hadn't felt the need to pursue greener pastures. At five feet and some few inches tall, Lester's head barely did stick out above the casket spray of white mums and baby's breath.

My fingers tightened on the slick metal edges of the casket cap, the part that opens to reveal the body lying inside, but no matter how much I tried, those fingers wouldn't take hold long enough for me to help Lester with the load. I knew I shouldn't have, but I slipped my right hand down to the handle on the head end where I stood and gave a pull. Lester straightened up so that he didn't look like he was trying to push a truck out of a mud hole, so I figured I must have relieved him of some of the burden.

I moved my hand back up to the pointed corners of the casket when we neared the narrow doorway that led from the wide main hallway of the funeral home to the chapel. As soon as I stopped pulling, I heard Lester grunt and saw his head drop back down below the spray.

The owner of the funeral home was adamant about where our hands should be when we rolled caskets, especially when there was any chance of damaging the merchandise by running into a doorjamb.

"Skin'll grow back," he liked to say. "Metal and wood won't." That's an adage I've not forgotten, but I don't ever recall seeing the owner with bloody knuckles, either.

If I grasped the sides of the casket where I was supposed to, only a couple of inches on either side kept my fingers from scraping the wooden doorframe. Lester's having to push made for slow going, but we slipped through the opening without a dent. We had another twenty feet before the narrow hallway opened up into the chapel, but I could already smell the tang of too many flowers that would be dead in three days. I reached down and pulled on the swing bar handle. Right on cue, Lester's head popped. As soon as I stepped backward into the chapel, I put my hands back where they were supposed to be.

The chapel at the funeral home could hold three-hundred people, and from the looks of what I saw over my left shoulder, we were at maximum capacity. I maintained a serious expression as I backed across the front of the large room, turned to my right, and straightened the casket up as soon as we hit our mark in front of the pulpit. The funeral directors took their time seating the family members; there must have been at least sixty or seventy sons, daughters, brothers, sisters, cousins, and assorted offspring.

Lester and I moved around to the front of the casket to open it for the service. I've always found it perversely remarkable that people want the casket open while the preacher preached. Seems to me that having to look at a loved one's earthly remains while trying to listen to what the preacher's saying might produce conflicting feelings. The collective moan of grief that rose up from the family when I pushed open the casket lid confirmed my point.

"Friends," the preacher said in his best funeral voice, "we've come to this memorial service to…"

Whenever I heard a minister refer to the funeral service as a memorial service, I wanted to scream, "Don't you see that body? It's not a memorial service if there's a body!" But I never did.

The service lasted about ninety minutes, and I could tell by the steady stream of people coming and going through the back doors to visit the restrooms, get water, answer their cell phones, or smoke a cigarette that these folks weren't used to staying in one place for any length of time unless they had fetters about their wrists or ankles. They must have been hell on their school teachers when they were younger.

When the last minister (there were three of them) launched the closing prayer, the funeral director motioned for us to take our places; it was time for the viewing. The viewing, or *run-around* as I've heard some people call it, usually comes at the end of the service. The casket's been open for nearly an hour with everybody watching the deceased for any sign of hope that this isn't really the end, and now the undertaker invites people to come up for one last look.

Lester and I led the way down the aisle, the director Hoke Harris right behind us. I took up a position at the head of the casket, and Lester stood by the foot end. Hoke started his slow commute back up the aisle of the chapel, stopping first at the front row opposite the family where the pallbearers sat, their fresh-out-of-the-pack Wal-Mart dress shirts and shiny patent leather shoes giving them fits.

"Would any of you gentleman care to see Mrs. Williams one final time?" I heard Hoke whisper.

Whether out of a genuine desire to get a look at Maxine Williams one more time or because they didn't know what to do and felt shamed into action by all the eyes fixed upon them, the pallbearers filed out of the pew and, hands shoved into their un-hemmed trouser pockets, filed past the open casket. Not a one of the men lifted his eyes to look at the dead woman lying swathed by the shiny taffeta interior. I motioned for the dumbstruck pallbearers to retake their seats as Hoke moved on toward the back of the chapel, pausing at each pew to ask if that group of mourners cared to walk the aisle to view the body one final time.

A few people made their way up to the casket before the cap was closed until the last trumpet sounds, but most folks stayed in their seats. Hoke finally got back around to the family, and that was a good thing; heads pivoting all around to see what was happening behind them, just about all of the family members gripped the pew in front of them to keep from rushing right out into the aisle. They were just itching to get up to that casket.

People deal with grief in their own ways. Some keep it all bottled up before the pain erupts one day in a destructive spewing of emotions. Some people let the tears out little-by-little until the well finally runs dry. And some folks take a more demonstrative approach, punctuating their sorrow with regular outbursts of crying, hollering, fainting, and foaming. Not only did the Williams family collectively ascribe to the latter category; they seemed to have perfected their art.

Hoke started with the eighth pew of immediate family members.

"It's time to come on up and pay your final respects to Mrs. Williams," he said.

Hoke intended to invite up one pew at a time, let them say their goodbyes, and send them back neatly to reclaim their seats while the next pew moved out. The first two rows of family members to walk the aisle up to Mrs. Williams's casket met Hoke's expectations: They visited the casket, cried some, and then returned to their pews. But the situation began to unravel when Hoke got to the children. The family members must have been sitting in order from eldest to youngest, the children in the front and muddled step-children behind them. Either way, when a young-looking fellow left his seat, the whole crowd moved with him as if they were all afraid he was going to take the last piece of chocolate cake.

The young man could have been a son or step-son, or he could have been a grandchild. Whoever he was, the churning mass swallowed him whole, and I don't remember seeing him after that. The eldest daughter, however, made herself well-known. Running, she rushed to the casket just ahead of the surging tide of family members. Situated right there at the open mouth of Maxine Williams's casket, she wrapped her meaty fingers around the front edge of the casket, leaned into it, and started hollering for her mama.

"Don't go, Mama!" she yelled.

The casket pitched forward as the daughter fell torso-first across her mama's body, and when the spray started to slide off the front, I reached out to steady the casket. Lester did the same from where he stood. If I hadn't grabbed the casket lid, it would have crashed down onto the woman's back.

Another daughter elbowed her way up to the front of the pack, and when she collapsed into the casket, I knew for sure we were about to have ourselves a mess of bodies littering the floor. Lester and I held the casket still, though, and Hoke pried his way through the crowd so he could offer support at the front.

"Ladies," I heard him whisper. "Ladies, it's time to go back to your pews."

One of the women raised her head and glared at Hoke before wailing even louder.

"We ain't gonna get very far like this," Hoke said to Lester over the din.

The preacher, who'd been standing beside me, stepped closer to the crying daughters and spoke. "Lisa, Shelly, it's time to get ready to go out to the cemetery. Y'all need to move on away so the undertakers can do their jobs."

When Lisa or Shelly or whoever she was failed to comply, the Baptist preacher, a man who looked as if he had eaten his share of fried chickens and bowls of banana pudding over the years, reached out a tender hand of support and touched the big woman's shoulder. With the sudden swiftness of a frog catching a lightning bug in midflight, she flung back her arm and slapped the preacher's hand away.

A man who, up to that point, had kept his distance at the rear of the pack saw the commotion and started chucking relatives out of his way to get to the casket. Before the preacher could say anything or react to the daughter's impassioned response to his soothing gesture of tactile compassion, a creature as tall as a sign post and as big around as a tractor tire grabbed the wide-eyed man of God by the front of the shirt and hoisted him off his feet.

"Don't you touch my wife!" he yelled.

"Vernon Tate, you put him down!"

"I ain't gonna let no man put his hands on you, Shelly!"

"He's the preacher, Vernon!"

Vernon eyed the dangling preacher. "That don't make no difference. A man's a man, and ain't no man, preacher or not, touching my wife."

By now the whole chapel seemed to have gone completely crazy. Babies cried, children ran around directionless, adults yowled and convulsed in choral unison, and the people sitting in the back half of the chapel, apparently not relatives of the deceased, stood as one and were now making their way out the back doors. The organist stopped her third trip through "Just as I Am," and the pall bearers tugged and fidgeted with their new funeral clothes.

"Excuse me, sir," said an in-control Hoke Harris. "You need to put that man down right now. Right now."

"And who's gonna make me, fancy boy? Not you."

Hoke retreated a little and offered his usual grin. "Well, no, I don't believe I'm going to make you do anything you don't want to do."

"You damn right you ain't," Vernon retorted.

Lester Polk, sixty-one years old and at least a foot and a quarter shorter than Vernon Tate, left his station at the foot of the casket and approached the giant as if the two of them were the only men in the room. "Mr. Tate," he said in his soft voice, a voiced laced with all the authority of one who might have a slingshot in his coat pocket. "This is your mother-in-law's funeral service. This chapel is a house of the Lord." Without turning around, he pointed back toward the flustered congregation. "Look out there at what you're doing to your friends and neighbors. They're running away scared." He motioned toward the preacher suspended in midair. "And that's the preacher you're holding, not some poolroom jackleg. You ought to be ashamed of yourself."

Vernon Tate cast his eyes down on the little man who dared talk to him that way. Any other man in any other place would find himself struggling to regain consciousness while he ran his tongue around gums that used to hold teeth.

Lester, his eyes locked on Vernon's, didn't waver a bit. Vernon squinted, glared at his wife Shelly who had taken hold of his free arm, and then looked at the preacher. Gently, as if he were laying a rose atop a grave, he lowered Reverend Murphy to the carpet.

Shelly returned her attention to her mother's corpse, but Hoke had already stepped between the woman and the casket and, extra careful not to touch Shelly Tate, was already urging the family back to their pews. I watched Lester reach out and lay a hand on the big man's arm.

"Thank you, Mr. Tate," he said. "You did the right thing."

Vernon Tate said nothing as he turned and joined his wife and family. They found their seats and waited.

"Let's go ahead and close the casket," Hoke said. "Quick, before anything else happens."

I folded the pink taffeta turn-out back into the casket before placing the overlay across Mrs. Williams's waist. Lester lifted the bulky spray, and I reached up to close the casket. As always, the crying intensified at the moment the lid was closed, and I knew the family of Maxine Williams had regained what was left of their composure.

"Did you see how big that man was?" Lester asked as he replaced the spray.

I whispered, "I did."

We made our way out into the sunlight of midafternoon where six uncomfortable pall bearers pushed the casket into the waiting hearse.

"Where's the minister?" I asked as Lester and I watched the family members crawl into their cars.

Lester looked around and shrugged.

We finally found the Reverend Murphy sitting inside the vestibule of the chapel, his face still red and his eyes watery.

"You all right, Preacher?" asked Lester.

"That is the last time I want anything to do with viewing the body after the service. I thought that man was going to kill me."

"No, we wouldn't have let it get that far," Lester said, patting the preacher's shoulder. "Upset daughters, jealous husbands, and the occasional scuffle come with the territory; you get used to it after a while."

Just Like Lazarus

The Reverend Calvert Moore prattled on in animated gestures during a crowded visitation. His hands jerked this way and that, hovering over his head before slicing diagonally through the air as he told his story, the same story he always told, to some poor soul too nice or too stupid to just smile and walk away. Pastor and owner of the Landfill Road Holiness Temple, Reverend Moore ran an auto detailing business on the side. From the motions of his hands, it looked like Preacher Moore might be practicing his "wax on, wax off" routine.

"My mama…," we heard him say.

Arnie, Clyde Combs, and I had the visitation shift that night. Seemed like every night we worked we had a visitation – a long one.

"He's at it again," said Clyde. "He's talking about his mama."

"And she was the dearest soul I ever knew. Why I bet right now she's looking down from heaven on her poor old son, grinning to beat the band because I've been preaching the Word for forty-four years in a row, and the devil knows to get on behind me."

Arnie rolled his eyes and started scanning the classified ads in a copy of *The State* lying on the desk. Clyde shoved his long, pre-arthritic hands into his trouser pockets and eased into the crowd standing by the back door. Pretty soon he would disappear, and we wouldn't see him again until closing time. I kept listening, moving closer to Reverend Moore so I could hear over the din coming from the hallway.

"But my daddy, he's in Hell," he continued. "Why, he used to drink and smoke and carouse all night. He was a sinner from head to toe. I remember Mama praying for him after us young 'uns went to bed, and I couldn't help but feel the hate rise up in my heart because of how he treated us all, Mama especially."

Then the tears started.

"But hate will eat you up inside, brothers and sisters. Mama was a saint if ever one walked the face of this earth, and she lived a solemn life after Daddy left us for the checkout girl at the Sky City." He wiped his eyes on the nose rag he kept in his coat pocket. "She prayed for him every day and every night, and when he finally died after he got himself stabbed at the County Line beer joint by that Sky City girl's husband who'd just got out on parole from the prison in Columbia, Mama said that she'd done all she could do. His soul was in the Lord's hands now."

He rubbed at his eyes some more before throwing back his head and studying the ceiling. "Oh, Lord," he cried, just loud enough for the folks in the hallway to hear, "you done good when you made my mama, but you dropped the mold and broke it to pieces when my daddy popped out."

Twenty or thirty people standing outside the stateroom hushed their own voices in order to hear Reverend Moore. Looked like just about all of them agreed with him, for their heads bobbed up and down and the smiles showed up on their faces like they were all too happy to hand over one tenth of their weekly paychecks to a man who drove a white Lincoln Continental and told the same story at every visitation and every funeral I had been on with him.

The telephone rang, and when I saw Clyde's head slipping down the staircase into the basement and Arnie talking to the dead man's brother, I figured I'd better answer it. When I put the receiver back into the cradle, I felt a presence before I even turned around.

"Good evening, brother," Reverend Moore said, and the words rolled off his lips so that he sounded like a politician at a court-house press conference.

"Evening, Reverend Moore."

At least six and half feet tall with a shock of jet black hair thick enough to belong to a teenaged Bedouin, Calvert Moore put his fingertips together in a gesture known as steepling and rocked back on the heels of his feet. His "steeple" was low enough on his chest that I figured his confidence level was high and he was feeling mighty good about himself.

"Tell me something, brother. Are you saved?"

I had willingly and joyfully engaged in theological discussions with Reverend Moore on several other occasions, but my heart just wasn't in in that night. "I am, same as I was last time you asked."

He looked down at me, his eyes scrunched up tight so he could measure my face with his hollow gaze. Finally, he leaned down as if he wanted to tell me a secret. "How do you know?"

My first reaction was to remind him of the oft misunderstood part of Jesus's Sermon on the Mount from Matthew 7:1 in which Jesus admonishes his listeners to avoid questioning the salvation of fellow Christians, but I wasn't sure he was actually judging my salvation yet.

"Same as you," was all I said.

Reverend Moore's steepled fingers narrowed and rose until his palms touched and the tips of his two index fingers rested against his top lip. After a moment to think about it, he said, "And how do you know about me?"

I already had my answer ready.

"I don't. But I would assume somebody who claims to be a man of God wouldn't fudge in the 'washed in the blood of the Lamb' department."

The preacher's eyes widened and his steeple closed around his Patrician's nose before he let out a frustrated breath and dropped his arms to his sides. "I suppose you go to church?"

"I do."

"Where?"

"You wouldn't know it if I told you," I said. "It's about twenty or so miles out of town."

"What denomination?"

"Presbyterian."

"Presbyterian?" He gave a little jump, pulled his hands back into a newly minted steeple, before reaching out and patting my shoulder the way a father might patronize his young son. "I'll be praying for you."

Before I could ask him what he meant by that, Arnie, who had been listening, stepped between us. "Reverend Moore," he said. "How are you tonight?"

"Just fine, Brother Arnie."

"Listen," Arnie continued, handing a pad and pen to the preacher. "I wonder if you would write down your order of service for us."

The preacher leaned over to bear down on the desk. "Boys, I've been thinking about Brother Jenkins yonder."

Steve Jenkins, a faithful member and tither of the Landfill Road Holiness Temple, was who brought all the people into the funeral home that night. He'd dropped dead of a heart attack two days earlier while he was working on his two-year-old John Deere lawn tractor.

Neither Arnie nor I said a word; we both knew it was best just to let Calvert Moore have his say. He looked up at us, the unmistakable gleam in his eye holding back a smile. He finished writing out the order of service.

"Yes, sir, at the funeral tomorrow, I think we'll raise Brother Steve right up out of that casket."

He straightened up, his eyes locked on mine. I wasn't sure I'd heard him right, so I kept my mouth shut. For a while, Arnie had been telling me to learn when to just be quiet, and I thought right then felt like as good a time as any. Arnie, though, couldn't let the remark pass. He laughed.

"Don't laugh," said Reverend Moore with all the seriousness of a pope. "That would blaspheme the name of the Lord, and you don't want no part of that, do you?"

Arnie lost his voice and started to mumble.

"Do you mean to tell me that you don't think God is powerful enough to raise Steve Jenkins right out of the casket if he wanted to?"

Arnie was smart enough not to fall for that one. "I suppose God can do anything he wants to do."

"You suppose? What do you mean, you suppose?" Reverend Moore threw up his arms and moved his hands about as if he was fanning hell's fire. "Goodness, me, boys. When we start supposing what the Almighty can and can't do, we may as well turn the world over to the communists and idolaters. Either God is all-powerful or he ain't."

He stopped and stared at Arnie.

Arnie fidgeted some more and said, "I guess God's all-powerful enough to do it."

"You guess?" The preacher put his hand on Arnie's shoulder the way he'd done me. "Friend, where do you go to church?"

"First Baptist Church."

"Baptist?" He said, and it was like déjà vu, but he didn't light into him the way he'd done me. "Brother, I would think a Baptist would have just a little bit more faith than say a …," and he looked my way, "… a Presbyterian."

I didn't have a chance to offer a retort, for he launched back into his resurrection theme.

"Boys, I think God wants me to bring Brother Steve up out of that casket tomorrow." His eyes sort of glassed over for a second. "I can feel the power washing through me."

This was really too much. "I have a question," I said.

"Go ahead, brother."

"Thank you. If Heaven is our everlasting reward, why would God want to send back somebody who's died and already gone to Heaven? Yes, I know it happened a couple of times in the Bible, but I don't understand why something like that would happen today."

Preacher Moore shook his head and looked at Arnie. "Presbyterians," he said, and the word came out with the same disgust that he might have used if he'd said *termites*.

"Are you a college boy?"

"I went to college."

He looked back at Arnie. "I figured as much. Listen here. Jesus raised ol' Lazarus as an example, a testimony to the power of God. Why if he could do that back in Bible days, he can surely do it today." He leaned in closed again. "It just takes a little faith."

Arnie sensed my eventual coming apart, and for the good of the funeral home, he decided to intervene. He took Reverend Moore to the side, and the two of them talked about the next day's service.

"You be there tomorrow, brother," he said to me as he sauntered away. "You'll see."

Steve Jenkins's funeral service turned out to be the unruly, raucous affair we all knew it would be. From the little vestibule of the funeral home chapel, I listened to the Reverend Calvert Moore talk about his dear, saintly mama and his pitiful, sinful daddy. He told about the day back in 1959 that he was saved as a teenager in a country church in Hartwell, Georgia, and he admitted a variety of slipups at the hands of conniving Judases and flaxen-haired Jezebels. Pretty soon a worn out accordion made its anticipated appearance, and he cried and sang "Beulah Land" and "Victory in Jesus" in a way that was almost pretty.

After the family had their final viewing, a part of the service that turned out to be disappointingly uneventful, I stood at the back of the chapel and watched as Reverend Moore stood over the open casket and prayed. He prayed for lost sinners in the congregation to get their hearts right with the Lord before it was too late, and he prayed for righteous mamas and wicked daddies all over the world. And then he did it. Right there in front of the family, the friends, and the undertakers, he asked God to raise up Steven Jenkins from that casket. He prayed hard, like a poor farmer begging for rain. Even though his back was to us all, I could imagine he had one eye cracked open so he could watch for movement. After several more fruitless attempts to talk God into one more resurrection, Reverend Moore said his Amen.

"Didn't quite work out the way you planned it, did it, Preacher?" I asked as the two of us stood by the back of the hearse waiting for the family members to move to their cars for the procession out to the cemetery.

He looked back at me, his black hair hanging heavier today than the previous night, his lanky frame bent over and weary from the passing storm. "Brother, where's your faith? I could have done it, all right, but God just wasn't ready to show this wicked world another miracle."

He patted me on the shoulder, smiled, and moved off toward his car. "Maybe next time, my little Presbyterian friend. Maybe next time."

Jesse Wept

Rosa Lee Cash had done her time. Daughter, sister, wife, mother, Christian. She worked her whole life in the now empty textile mill to put her two daughters through tech school. When her husband succumbed to the cancer, she took an ecclesiastical view of things: "'Twas his season." Grandchildren had padded barefoot around her kitchen; great-grands had slept in her arms. Neighbors missed her. Church members couldn't recall a time when Rosa Lee wasn't in her regular pew at the Rocky Branch Pentecostal Holiness Church.

Jesse wept.

"She'll be missed here on Earth," the preacher proclaimed, "but her name's been added to the role up yonder."

Jesse wept.

Rosa Lee's daughter, a solid woman who lived off Highway 28 in the house next to her mama, turned her head toward the weeping.

"'In my house are many mansions,'" the preacher read. "'Were not so, I would have told you.'"

Jesse tried not to look directly at Mrs. Cash's daughter, but the stoic woman groped for her eyes. Then she found them. Jesse raised her eyebrows and pursed her lips before turning her attention to a lonely speck on her skirt. Her thoughts shifted to a dark house awaiting her solitary return when the preacher finally said "Amen."

"'I go to prepare a place for you.'"

Jesse wept and saw that Peony Cash Osborn had turned back

around, and even from behind the woman, Jesse could tell she was staring at Rosa Lee's full casket up there in front of the pulpit.

"'Yea, though I walk through the valley of the shadow of death…'"

After a time, the preacher finally offered his closing prayer, and when it was over, the organist played "I Surrender All."

Two undertakers trotted down the aisle. One closed the casket while the other hoisted the spray of white mums and daisies, and a collective burst of grief issued from the family.

Jesse wept.

Peony Osborn stood, and she and her sister and their assembled brood followed Rosa Lee Cash's white casket out into the light of August.

Jesse waited until everyone left the building before forsaking the pew near the middle of the chapel where she always sat by herself. Instead of joining the gaggle of mourners, she slipped unobserved through a small side door. She found herself in the whispery main hall of the funeral home, where unoccupied staterooms awaited the inescapable repose of future guests.

"Thank you for your participation," murmured Hoke Harris, the smiling funeral director. He offered a plain white envelope. "Back at 4:00?"

"Planning to."

Before Jesse slipped the envelope into her shirt pocket without looking at it, she rubbed it between her thumb and index finger; she knew the feel of a one-hundred dollar bill.

Jesse Metters was a professional – a professional mourner.

The funeral home called her when they wanted real tears of grief and despair. Jesse was a seat-filler, a ringer, a warm body. Jesse's singular presence provided the pretense of comfort.

Jesse walked home alone.

Jesse wept for a living.

Jesse wept.

Ever with the Lord

Thirty-year old Sammy Eugene Sibley pointed the gun and shot at his wife. He missed. Wendy Martin Sibley aimed her husband's Remington 12-gage pump, the one he kept behind the seat of his truck, at her husband's heart. She didn't miss.

They had the funeral on a Tuesday. It rained that day. I was on the flowers for the service, and what a day to haul flowers. Raining. Crowded funeral home chapel. A van that would be so crammed with floral tributes that I felt certain the only thing I would unload at the muddy cemetery would be flower-petal confetti.

What I gathered from the many conversations the night before during the visitation was that Sammy Sibley had always been, well, a jackass. You know the type. Got in trouble all the way through school – gave his elementary school teachers fits until they got wise enough to promote him on to the next grade just to rid themselves of a boy so hardheaded that no paddling, no warning, and no suspension would straighten him out. He spent most of his high school years sitting in something they call In-School Suspension, which basically meant the boy missed all there was to learn about reading, writing, and arithmetic; they kicked him out when he was eighteen. He did, though, learn how to steal cars, smoke pot, and beat up on his girlfriends. That's how he met Wendy.

Wendy brought her own stack of troubles to their rocky marriage, so it wasn't until the baby was born that she figured she'd better start fighting back. Sammy let up on her for a while, but when little Aaron Sibley was six months old, Sammy slid back into his old ways. Wendy was bright enough to see that a pattern emerged from Sammy's abusive mayhem: get drunk, pass out, wake up mad at the world, punch on Wendy.

"The hell with this," she said.

So she started hitting back. The first time Wendy defended herself, she caught her husband with a right haymaker to the temple. The blow didn't knock him out, but it did knock him on his butt. He sat right there on the living room floor with his legs spread out in a V and his arms dangling between them puppet-style. He cocked his head up and squinted his watery eyes.

"What the hell did you do that for?" he asked her.

Wendy examined her stinging knuckles as if she were seeing them for the first time in her life. Unexpectedly she'd found her voice through action. "I ain't your punching bag," she said. "Stop hitting me."

And Sammy did stop hitting Wendy for a little while. In fact, whenever he got near Wendy, he kept himself at arm's length away from her, for he now saw little Wendy Martin through addled eyes. But you know that familiarity breeds presumption, and presumption breeds complacency. Sammy soon grew complacent. Sammy remembered his old self and missed that S.O.B.

It was the old Sammy, a self-satisfied Sammy, who shouted for his wife to come out to the yard one evening.

"Get out here!" he hollered.

She walked to the screen door, little Aaron on her hip. "What you want?"

"Put the boy down and come here."

Wendy looked at her son, and right there she realized that little Aaron Michael Sibley was going to turn out just like his daddy. She shook her head. When the boy was secured in his playpen, she stepped out onto the porch.

"What?"

Sammy started a fight with his wife. It was about money or beer or presumed infidelity or checkers — it really didn't matter. He yanked her off the porch by the head of her hair, throwing her clear across the yard.

"What you gonna do?" he taunted. "You gonna hit me?"

Before Wendy could shake the cobwebs from her head, Sammy plucked her up by her hair again and hit her with a closed fist right in the mouth. Wendy dropped to the ground, her tongue swishing around the metallic taste of blood. Back in the house, the baby started crying.

Wendy didn't cry, though. She stood up and opened the door to Sammy's old Ford. What she sought was a napkin or a rag to press to her split lip, but what she found was the butt end of the shotgun. Out of the corner of her eye, she watched Sammy snake his way to her left. Slow and steady she was when she pulled that shotgun from the truck.

Sammy saw what his wife had in her hand, and he couldn't help but laugh. "Put that gun down. You know you don't want to start playing with guns now."

"I told you I wasn't going to let you hit me again."

"So you're gonna shoot me now? I don't think so."

Wendy raised the gun so that the barrel pointed to the dirt in front of Sammy's feet. She watched her husband where he stood fifteen feet away, and she was scared. "I don't want to shoot you. Don't make me. All I want is to get Aaron and go to my mama's."

Sammy took a step. "You ain't going nowhere." He took another step. "And I'm gonna make you eat that gun," he said. "Ain't nobody pointing no gun at me and getting away with it."

Wendy held the shotgun in her right hand, her fingers wrapped around the breech block and the trigger guard, and with her left, she racked the fore stock and chambered a round of buckshot. That done, she raised the gun so that it was level with Sammy's chest. "Don't make me shoot you, Sammy. I mean it." Her voice was calm, soft, full of resignation.

His right foot already groping for another step, Sammy thought better and retreated a yard or two. His voice lost its usual playfulness and took on a tone of menace. "When I get my hands on you, woman, I'm gonna beat the tarnation out of you."

Wendy stepped out in front of the truck. She raised the stock of the gun, the recoil pad firm against her shoulder, and looked down the barrel with her right eye until she had the front sight lined up with the shirt pocket over Sammy's left chest. "I just want to go," she pleaded.

Sammy Eugene Sibley knew that he'd been beat. But instead of stepping aside and letting his wife collect their son and go to her mother's house just up the road, he pulled a small .22 caliber revolver from his back pocket. Without a word, he raised the gun, pointed it in the vicinity of his wife's head, and jerked the trigger.

The bullet whizzed past Wendy's head and punched a hole in the pickup's windshield, but she didn't move so much as an inch. Employing a fluidity that she had developed shooting with her daddy when she was a little girl, Wendy squinted her eye and squeezed the trigger. A thunderous boom shattered the afternoon stillness, and when the echo finally subsided, Sammy Sibley lay bleeding in the front yard, where he sucked in his final breaths with little fuss.

Wendy's mama and daddy walked behind her down the aisle of the funeral home chapel. Her son still too young to understand what was happening, she held the baby close to her chest, fearing he might float away back to Heaven if she loosened her grip. Sammy's mama, her heart black with grief and hate, decided to sit in the back of the chapel, as far away from her daughter-in-law as she could get and still be in the same room. People filled every pew, lined the walls, and waited in the vestibule. The place was packed.

"Let's start with a prayer," the Reverend Charles Hart said once the family sat down and he'd seated the congregation.

Reverend Hart had spent fifty-one years preaching God's word, starting in York County, South Carolina. The worshipers in little white clapboard building on Highway 161 near a rough spot in the road called Tirzah found themselves bereft of a pastor when their own man of God took off to Charlotte with a dancer he'd met in Rock Hill. Charles Hart, a drinker and a fighter and a sinner and a Baptist for as long as anyone could remember, found the Holy Spirit and surrendered himself to the ministry. He was nineteen years old.

Life's many and varied pathways directed Reverend Hart to this moment when he stood before the family of Sammy Eugene Sibley to offer words at the dead man's funeral sermon. He started the way most preachers do, his heart heavy and his words light. Scripture seemed to dominate his thoughts, but the passages came out cluttered and random.

"'In my Father's house are many mansions…'"

"'But I would not have you to be ignorant, brethren, concerning them which are asleep …'"

"'Yea, though I walk through the valley of the shadow of death, I will fear no evil…'"

"'And the dead in Christ shall rise first…'"

It was that last passage, the one about the dead in Christ and those who remain on earth joining Christ in the clouds when the final trumpet sounds, that caused the Reverend Charles Hart to lose his place. Something about the "dead in Christ" got to him. The old preacher took off his glasses, pulled a wrinkled white handkerchief from his coat pocket, and wiped his face. He leafed through the pages of his worn Bible, his tired eyes searching for some revelation. Minutes passed, but Reverend Hart could not recover.

He looked down at the closed casket below the pulpit, the generic white flowers – carnations, mums, and baby's breath – wilting in the humidity. The man's eyes rolled up slowly until they found the eyes of Wendy Sibley. The widow's eyes, deep blue and ice cold as the underside of a glacier, held the preacher's gaze, their uninvited truths divulging to him the words he sought.

"I can't do this," Reverend Hart said, and he closed his Bible.

His bloodshot eyes, their sclera a jaundice yellow, began to water; he turned his head to the right until Wendy Sibley forfeited her grip on his gaze.

"I don't care what any of us think," the Reverend Hart shouted. "Sammy Sibley is in Hell, plain as day!"

A tremor of disbelief rolled across the congregation. Ladies' hands touched their lips, men's foreheads turned to deep furrows, and sluggish children craned their necks at the thundering word *Hell*.

Those of us waiting sleepy-eyed in the vestibule perked up. I'd never seen funeral men stir so quickly from their napping. Arnie, who was driving the hearse that day, jumped to his feet and turned up the volume on the wall speaker.

"That man is layin' in this casket right now because he was

meaner than a cotton mouth snake! He beat is wife! He didn't work. He didn't provide a loving home for his little boy. Sammy Sibley was thirty years old and still acted like an irresponsible teenager. He drank too much beer, smoked too much dope, and I hear he'd started making meth in the little shed behind his house!"

Preacher Hart was just getting started. "Sammy is dead today because he tried to kill his wife! He tried to shoot her, but the good Lord wasn't ready for her to go. No, sir. Jesus himself said in the book of Matthew that if you live by the sword, you'll die by the sword. Sammy Sibley lived by the sword. He picked fights and took advantage of people. And when he realized he couldn't take on no man, he turned his meanness toward his little wife." The old preacher shook his head. "But she wasn't gonna have none of that. No, sir. She showed him what she could do. God used her to fulfill his eternal purpose three days ago."

Sammy's mother had already stormed out of the chapel. Her silent misery hard and strong enough to send her to the back pew, this new wound proved more than she could take.

"But what I want you people to know today is that God offers eternal life to those who believe, to those of us who are born again and live our lives for Christ." Then he looked at Wendy Sibley, her face contorted in confusion, her eyes wide with disbelief. "You know that your husband wasn't saved, and you know that he's in Hell right now."

A backdrop of murmuring set the stage for what happened next. Wendy Sibley stood up from the front pew and pointed a shaky finger at the preacher. "How dare you say my husband ain't in Heaven? He was a good man, and I'd take him back right now." She snatched up her sleeping son from the pew. "You're the one who ain't no true Christian. You're the one who can just go … to … Hell!"

By now we had the doors open at the back of the chapel; with so many people walking in and out, we figured no one would mind if we went ahead and propped open the doors before the minister's final prayer. I looked up to see an indomitable Wendy Sibley marching straight for me, her blonde hair hanging in her face and her slender legs pumping so hard to get out of there that her already short skirt had risen halfway up her thigh.

"Get out of my way," she ordered.

I stepped aside and watched Wendy, followed by most of the immediate family, kick open the heavy door that led outside and proceed to her car. Coy Franklin, the director in charge of the service, tried to get the widow's attention.

"Mrs. Sibley," Coy called after her, "we have a family car right here for you."

"Forget the family car," she said without looking back, but she didn't say *forget*. "I'm getting out of here."

A cacophony of voices, some angry, some confused, some just plain weary, resounded through the vestibule as the chapel emptied. Down front, the Reverend Charles Hart, still standing motionless with his arms propping him up on the lectern, was getting an earful from several men whose relation to the wife or the deceased remained a mystery.

"Arnie," Coy said. "Take junior here, and the two of you go down and get the casket. See if you can rescue the preacher before those fellows strangle him." He turned toward the crowd gathered beside the hearse outside in the rain. "Let me see if I can find the pallbearers."

The casket seemed to be the only thing keeping the three men who were yelling obscenities at Reverend Hart from grabbing the trembling man and beating the tar out of him right there under the cross. Arnie, who often found himself at a loss for words, took umbrage at the men's treatment of the minister and inserted himself between the men and the casket.

"Men," said Arnie, "I'm going to have to ask you all to step back. It's time for us to go to the cemetery, and we need to move this casket."

"We're pallbearers," one of them said.

"Good," Arnie replied. "Go wait for us on the front steps."

Without another word, the men turned and walked away from us up the aisle.

"You all right, Preacher?" I asked.

Charles Hart stood up straight and cleared his throat. "In all my years preaching the Gospel, I have never seen anything like that."

Arnie shook his head, a grin spreading across his lips. "What did you think was going to happen when you told the family that the dead man was in Hell?"

"To be honest with you, I don't rightly know." He mopped the back of his head with the handkerchief. "But I don't guess it was that."

"The preacher telling you that your husband, your son, or your brother is in Hell is probably pretty tough for a person to hear," I offered. "But admitting that the preacher's right is probably a whole lot tougher."

The preacher shook his head. "I reckon I shouldn't have said it. Nobody really knows for sure but the good Lord."

"Well, what's done is done, Preacher," said Coy Franklin as he walked up to us. "You can't unring the bell." He held his hand out, indicating that the minister should lead the way up the aisle.

"Oh, no," Reverend Hart said. "I'm done. Y'all can have the rest of this mess of a service. Those people would be liable to hang me up by my toes and beat me with their shoes if I show up at the graveyard." He grabbed his Bible and headed toward the back door. "I don't know if that boy is ever with the Lord, but I ain't hanging around to find out."

Jesus Called

When florists, like the rest of us, find something that works, they stick with it. So, even though I became acquainted with the "Jesus Called" floral arrangement on my third day as an apprentice funeral director, Arnie insisted that the kitschy cemetery piece had been around many, many years. At first glance, there was nothing remarkable about the gaudy, greenery-filled spray atop its rusty, recycled, metal stand. It stood right there in the flower room with the rest of the floral tributes being delivered by several local florists, and I counted it as little more than just another piece I needed to tag and send up to the main viewing floor.

"There's a plastic telephone on it," I said.

Arnie stepped out of the weary freight elevator and grinned. "Jesus called."

I looked at the dangling ribbon that bore those exact words written in glitter. "But it's a child's toy. On a funeral spray. That's tacky."

Arnie pushed past me and picked up a small peace lily. "But people love it," he said. "You watch. That spray will sit up there on the floor for visitation tonight, and people will fawn all over it. Then in the next few weeks, we'll see more and more of them popping up." He stapled a numbered tag to the card. "I'm telling you – people eat that stuff up."

After I stapled a tag to the "Jesus Called" card, the name read Chadwick, I looked at the cheap telephone. It was an old fashioned model, the kind with a rotary dial and a spiral chord. The pink telephone served as the arrangement's centerpiece, and I wondered if that was why the spray didn't contain any more flowers than it did. I put the wobbly spray on the elevator and laughed to myself: There was always something else to learn.

The next day, Coy Franklin put both Arnie and me on the Chadwick service in the funeral home chapel. I was on the flowers again, and Arnie had the hearse. Once everyone processed into the chapel, I took my seat in the vestibule and began working a crossword puzzle to pass the time. I don't know what it was that caused me to look up from number 37 down, but suddenly I found myself listening to the sermon. The Reverend Calvert Moore, the minister who had tried unsuccessfully to raise Steve Jenkins from his casket several months earlier, officiated, and he was talking about his mama.

I listened to the same old story about his dear, saintly mother and his wicked, eternally damned father. But then he stopped talking. I looked at Arnie and Coy, but Arnie was asleep and Coy had his nose inside an old church bulletin, so I went over to the chapel doors for a look. Pulling open one of the doors about an inch, I saw Reverend Moore holding up a cell phone and squinting his eyes to make out the little screen.

"I'm sorry, but y'all are gonna have to excuse me. I can't make out the number." He looked at the family. "I'm gonna have to take this call."

A murmur ran through the crowd as mourners looked on in disbelief at a minister taking a cell phone call right in the middle of a service.

"Hello," Reverend Moore said, his voice a nasal twang. "Who is this?"

I watched as the preacher listened, his eyebrows arched and his lips pursed for effect.

"This is who?" he said, and he held the phone at arm's length so he could get a good look at it.

The members of Effie Chadwick's family leaned forward in their seats, their ears hanging on the preacher's every word. Even the babies and toddlers grew quiet. Reverend Moore turned his attention to the family, his right hand extending the phone toward them.

"Y'all ain't gonna believe this: It's Jesus! Jesus is calling!"

Like a sudden strong wind, a collective wail issued from the family members. Mrs. Chadwick's daughter, tears streaming from her face, stood straight up and threw her body over the railing at the front pew. Her heels' hitting the pew was the only thing that kept her from flopping on over. Those quiet babies began to stir, and their voices soon joined in the echo of grief and surprise.

"Hush, now!" Reverend Moore ordered. "Y'all settle down. I can't hear Jesus."

And as if somebody had cut off a spigot, the family settled down.

"Yes, sir. Yes, sir. I'm still here." He listened. "We know she's with you." He cupped his hand over the mouthpiece and directed his attention back toward the distraught family. "Jesus says your mama is sitting there with him, right there at his feet."

Pandemonium broke out again, and once again the daughter lunged forward, and this time her husband grabbed her around the shoulders to keep her from going right over the rail. A man on the second row stomped his feet and spun around, his hands pointed up in the air and his eyes glued to the ceiling. A man a couple rows back hollered "Jesus!" and two women elsewhere shouted "Glory!"

"Y'all be quiet, now!" the preacher yelled. "This is Jesus I got here on the phone."

He waited for the crowd to come to order; they took their time about it, though, for having Jesus on the line was about as close as many of them had come to any type of one-on-one contact with the Savior.

"I'm still here," Reverend Moore said from behind the pulpit. "I understand. I sure do. I think that would be a fine thing, I really do."

Cupping his hand over the phone, Reverend Moore looked at the daughter and the husband who held her. "Jesus is gonna let me talk to your mama."

All three of Effie Chadwick's daughters, at least one son, and several grandchildren rushed the front of the chapel. The crowd bumped against the casket and flowers, not about to let a dead body stand in their way.

"Mama!" one of the daughters screamed. "It's me, Cindy, Mama!"

The lone son started chucking flowers out of his way, but Reverend Moore was not to be outdone by a common lout in an ill-fitting sport coat.

"Miss Effie." Reverend Moore cooed into the phone, cradling the Nokia as if it were a baby. "This is Reverend Calvert Moore, your preacher. Yes, ma'am. Your family's all here, gathered 'round the altar."

This time the preacher's words, spoken softy and tenderly to the heavenly remains of Effie Chadwick, brought an immediate and profound hush over the chapel. Once again ears perked up and eyes widened as all focus and attention were directed toward Reverend Moore.

For thirty long seconds, he listened in earnest without uttering a word. Pretty soon his eyes got all watery and an errant tear slipped down his cheek.

"Your mama says that she's glad to be with Jesus. She says she don't hurt no more and that all the bad that ever happened in her life, all the sin and disappointment, all the grief and strife, it's been washed away by the blood of Jesus." He paused for effect as the hallelujahs resounded through the chapel. "And she's with your daddy. Praise the Lord, your daddy's right there with your mama and Jesus, and they're laughing and singing and dancing." Reverend Moore wiped his eyes. "I wish I could say that my daddy was in Heaven."

"Mama!" cried out Cindy.

"Come back!" begged another daughter.

"Let me talk to my mama!" said the son, and I believe Reverend Moore took a step back.

"Y'all listen," he said. "Listen. She don't want to come back. She says she wouldn't come back if Jesus hisself were to bring her down and set her right here in front of us. She's home. She's with Jesus, basking in the sunshine of Glory!"

Like people used to being told what to do by important others in authority, the Chadwicks calmed down and began to whimper like babies. They sniffed and snorted, ragged and worn Kleenex tissues dissolving between their fingers.

"Can't we just talk to her for a minute?" Cindy begged. "I got things I need to say to her. She left too soon."

Calvert Moore listened into the phone. He shook his head. "Jesus says she's gone on, now. She's running up a street of gold with your daddy. She's rejoicing with the angels and singing songs." He ended the call. "You all go ahead and have a seat."

All the members of the family returned to their seats, their eyes puffy and their breathing stopped up with sadness. Reverend Moore broke out his guitar and plucked out "Beulah

Land" amidst his own tears. When he was finished, he looked as bad as the family. He blew his nose on a rag from his coat pocket, and then led us all in a closing prayer.

"Come on down, boys," he instructed us when he'd finished praying. "I'm turning it back over to the undertakers, now."

The Reverend Moore, sniffing as he walked, led the pallbearers to the vestibule and the waiting Coy Franklin. Arnie and I rolled out the casket, the sobbing family on our heels. The pallbearers loaded the casket into the hearse, and that was when I saw Reverend Moore lingering on the other side of the open hearse door. His lips, neither downturned in a frown nor curled upward in a smile, spread out across his dark face. He took the little phone from his pocket.

"You can't beat a phone call from Jesus, boys," he said.

I shook my head. "It sure did seem to get to them."

This time the preacher grinned. "Gets 'em every time, boys" he said with a wink. "Every time."

Things Happen

Even though Melvin Hall had been driving cars since before his voice changed, the intricacies of modern automotive innovations further slowed his already wilting reflexes. Antilock brakes? "Too tight on the stop," he complained. Air conditioning? "You're supposed to be hot and uncomfortable in a car." Fuel injection? "Where's the damn carburetor on this thing?" Electric locks? "Electric? There ain't no wires running to this car. It's gas." The electric locks were what finally made Melvin retire at age eighty after fifty-six years in the funeral business.

Melvin was driving the second car, and he and Hoke Harris, the funeral director in charge of that service, were getting ready to pick up the family at their house.

"Follow me, Melvin," Hoke said. "And don't get too close. This time."

This time was a reference to Melvin's last excursion behind the wheel of one of the funeral home's limousines. He'd followed right behind Hoke on their way to collect the family for a service at a church, and Melvin, while fiddling with the radio, nearly slammed into the backend of Hoke's car.

Hoke stopped short of climbing into his car and hollered at Melvin. "And leave that radio alone this time."

Three funeral coaches, three limousines, two flower vans, two station wagons, and three lead cars comprised the funeral home's rolling stock. The main funeral home building, a six-bay garage with storage rooms on either end, and a small storage building made up the organization's fixed assets. Main Street, teaming with traffic at all hours of the day, ran along in front of the funeral home, and the constant flow of automobiles regularly made exiting the parking lot a test of will and dexterity. Adding to the confusion was the traffic light at the corner of Brown Street, which bordered the northern edge of the property, and Main Street; the duration of the green light in the three-light cycle was notoriously short.

Hoke pulled out of the parking lot onto Brown Street and proceeded to the light. As he'd been instructed, Melvin followed, but kept his vehicle back a safe distance. To their right, the cars lined up for the 2:00 o'clock funeral's procession sat empty. The red light turned to green, and Hoke edged the limo into the intersection. By the time the oncoming cars had made their left turn, the signal was yellow. Hoke made his left turn just in time. Melvin pressed the accelerator to the floor, the big Cadillac lurching forward and out of the way of the mechanical steeds bounding out of the gate upon the light change.

"That was close," he muttered to himself as he slowed his vehicle to follow Hoke.

The fact that it was almost 3:30 in the afternoon made the heavier-than-usual Friday traffic worse. The funeral was at four o'clock, and Hoke needed to have the family back just in time to process down the aisle. Several blocks up from the funeral home, Hoke activated his turn signal and let the big car slip into the left turn lane. Melvin followed. This particular intersection was busier than usual, and Hoke and Melvin found themselves inching up only a couple of cars at time during each light change. Red – Green – Yellow. Move up two cars. Wait.

Aside from being persistently impatient and embarrassingly loud, Melvin's other distinguishing characteristic was his proclivity for profanity. Not the biggies: Never the F word. Never any abuse of the Lord's name. No, Melvin was a "What the hell?" and "Damn this" and "Damn that" kind of guy. But he was a happy swearer, a pleasant practitioner of unimaginative language more than an angry slinger of verbal abuses.

"What the hell's taking so long?" he muttered to himself.

That was the moment Melvin's impatience overrode his judgment. Shaking his head in dismay at their inability to move forward, Melvin pushed the gear shifter to park, threw open his door, and exited his vehicle. Hands on his hips, he marched up to Hoke's car and knocked on the window.

Hoke Harris looked out the driver's side window to see Melvin standing there. "What are you doing out of your car, Melvin?"

"I want to know why we're not moving!" he said, his voice loud and screechy like an owl. He waved his hands over his head. "We're just sitting here!"

Hoke couldn't believe this was happening. "Get back inside your car, Melvin. The light's turning green now."

Melvin looked up at the light, saw the line of cars beginning to move, and grinned. "Okay."

He walked happily back to his car, completely oblivious to the stares and soundless comments issuing from behind tempered windshields as drivers passed by. Pleased that the line of cars was about to move, Melvin grasped the door handle and pressed the chrome button. Nothing happened. He tried it again. Nothing. Still not understanding the problem, he stepped back to the middle door and tried it. Nothing. The back door – nothing. All three doors on the passenger side refused to admit him as well.

"I'll be damned," Melvin said to himself. "The doors are locked."

Hoke looked into his rear-view mirror and saw a bewildered Melvin standing outside his car with his hands on his hips. "What now?" he grumbled.

"Melvin," he hollered, opening his car door and leaning as far out as he could without toppling over onto the pavement. "What in the world are you doing?"

Melvin walked toward Hoke. "I locked my keys in the car."

"Locked the keys in the car?" Hoke repeated. "You've got to be kidding me."

Melvin shook his head. "Nope." A big grin took up his whole face, eyes and all. "I sure enough locked 'em in there. Didn't mean to, but I did it." He leaned down as if he might whisper something in Hoke's ear. "You got a spare set on you so we can get moving?"

"A spare set? Are you serious? No, I don't have a spare set. The spare set's hanging on the wall back at the funeral home, Melvin."

By this point the light had turned red and irritated drivers had started pulling into the right-hand lane and around the stranded family car. Because many of the drivers recognized that the vehicles belonged to the funeral home, they restrained their tongues.

"Well," Melvin chuckled, "looks like we got a predicament here."

"Get out of the road and stand over there on the sidewalk," Hoke ordered. Traffic was starting to back up as curious drivers in the far right lane slowed down to gawk at the comical spectacle impeding movement in the turn lane. Because cars trying to get around the stranded limo in the turn lane had to swing out right, drivers in the center lane of traffic couldn't move. Hoke could see that this situation could turn ugly at any moment. "I'm going back to the funeral home to get the other set of keys," he said over the cacophony of car horns. "Don't get run over."

Watching Hoke and the limo speed through the intersection and head back to the funeral home three blocks away, Melvin waited patiently on the sidewalk, his hands behind his back. His own car loitered in the turn lane, the engine's purr barely discernable beneath the traffic's roar.

"Get that car out of the way!" yelled a man in a black truck.

"Sorry, my friend," Melvin answered with a shrug. "Locked the keys in the car."

"Who locks their keys in a running car at a red light?" shouted another passerby.

Melvin raised his hands in the air, elbows bent, palms toward the sky. "It happens."

"Are you some kind of idiot?" someone asked.

Thin, disheveled Melvin, his black pants bunching up around his scuffed shoes, his tie crocked, his white shirt stained with too many coffee spills, rocked back and forth on the balls of his flat feet. "No," he replied. "Just a human. Things happen."

"Don't listen to them," a kindly woman offered. "It could happen to anybody."

Melvin smiled. "It's all right," he shouted as she drove past. "When you get to be my age, you learn to take it all in stride. Things happen."

The comments from the passing motorists who had to slow down amidst the confusion ranged from compassionate and understanding to downright nasty.

"What's the trouble?"

Melvin looked around to see a uniformed city police officer standing beside him. The young patrolman, his car parked in the Burger King parking lot behind them, had a smile on his face as he stared at the idling limousine.

"That a funeral home car?"

"It is."

The man laughed. "What happened?"

Once again Melvin grinned and shrugged. "Damnedest thing. The keys got locked inside."

"You the driver?"

"Yep."

"How did you come to not be inside your vehicle at a traffic light?"

Melvin shook his head. "Things happen. I'm only human."

Before the policeman could continue his investigation of what was turning out to be one serious traffic debacle, Hoke pulled into the Burger King parking lot and jumped out of his car. "Here," he said, pushing the spare key into Melvin's hand. "Go move your car before anything else can go wrong."

Dodging and weaving through the traffic like the sure-to-be-squished frog from the Frogger video game, Melvin finally reached his car. With Hoke and the representative of the city's finest looking on, he fumbled with the key before finally getting it to work. Instead of jumping into the driver's seat, throwing the car into gear, and fleeing the scene the way any normal person would, he stood there with the door open.

"Well," he hollered, "looks like we're back in business."

"Shut up and move that car out of the way," the woman in the car behind him screamed. "I need to pick my kid up."

"Hold your horses, lady," Melvin yelled. "I'm trying."

"Melvin, be quiet and go," Hoke said. "There's a procession about to leave the funeral home any minute. You need to get that car out of the way!"

But it was too late. Headlights blazing, the funeral procession rounded the curve. The owner, the boss, was driving the lead car, and his eyes locked on Melvin's. Melvin stood beside the conspicuous limo that was blocking traffic, and as soon as the lead car drew even with his own car, he ceremoniously placed his right hand over his heart.

"Get your hand away from your heart, you boob," Hoke called out.

"I locked the keys in the car!" Melvin yelled to the owner, and then he held up the spare key in his left hand. "But we're good now." He was grinning like a cat eating bubblegum out of a hair brush. "We got it under control!"

While Hoke looked at a faded burger wrapper on the ground, he could feel the eyes of his employer bearing down on him. The long line of cars following the hearse to a little church cemetery somewhere out in the northern part of the county finally passed out of sight. As soon as the last car cleared the intersection, car horns began to break the silence.

"Let's go!" someone shouted.

"Get out of the way!"

"What's the problem up there?" yelled another.

"I'm ready when you are, Hoke," Melvin said. "You ready?"

Hoke Harris had had all he could take. "Just get the car out of the lane, Melvin."

Melvin smiled at a child in the backseat of an SUV; the little boy was sticking his tongue out and giving Melvin the finger. "Cute kid," Melvin chuckled.

"Just go!" Hoke screamed. "It's time to go!"

"Settle down now, Hoke," said Melvin. "Settle down. Like my mama always used to say, 'Things happen.'"

The Cemetery

The Savior

The casket was too big for the grave. Well, to tell the truth, it wasn't so much too big for the hole as the casket was too wide to fit between the supports of a standard lowering device, a back-saving work of art used to lower the casket into the grave. The dead woman was pretty big, and the funeral director told the family that they needed to purchase an oversized casket for her interment. But they knew she was a big woman, and they complied, for what did they know about such funeral particulars anyway?

That it happened to be raining that day didn't help matters. Rivulets of dirty orange water were already streaming underneath the tent when the family decided to leave the little country church cemetery and go back home. What the family didn't know was that the grave would begin filling up with water before long. The gravediggers know this all too well, and they understood that the sooner they got Mrs. Littlejohn under three or so feet of earth, the better off everyone would be.

"We're gonna have to lower this thing by hand, said the man in charge, a pot-bellied gravedigger named George. Then he withdrew three rolled canvas straps from the pocket of his soiled overalls.

I looked around. Three straps meant six people: three men on either side of the casket who would hold the straps and lift the casket into the air. Someone would then pull away the reinforced, one-inch-thick piece of plywood so we could lower the casket into the grave. The concept was simple, but we had a problem: There were only six of us, we were a man short, and we were at least eight miles out in the middle of nowhere.

A keen-eyed George had already noticed this fact. "How big did you say this here woman is?" he asked me.

"She's at least three hundred," I replied. "Maybe three and some change."

For my part, I felt pretty sure I was giving the deceased the benefit of the doubt. She'd been a lot of woman.

"Yep," he said. "And how much does this casket weight?"

I thought. "About two hundred, give or take."

He shook his head, removed an old blue rag from his pocket, and cleared his red nose. "That's a lot of weight for only four or five of us to manage, especially with all this water. I reckon we'd be a lot better off if we had a seventh man to pull out the grave board."

I knew he was right. Many times had I helped lift a regular-sized casket using those straps, only to have them slip through my hands with a blistering burning. Our prospects of utilizing the services of an additional person that far out in the middle of nowhere, however, were about as good as the dead Mrs. Littlejohn getting out of her tall and wide casket to help us.

"Why not lift up the casket and set it over here on the ground?" another digger mused.

"No," I said. "I don't think the family would be too happy if we set mama's casket in the mud."

We, though, were standing in at least an inch of orange Carolina mud, the thick stuff that sticks to shoes and somehow manages to work its way up clean trouser legs, onto the cuffs of finely starched shirts, and could miraculously travel beneath undershirt and all to where a single, tell-tale smudge on a belly or the back of the arm might haunt the victim with its almost spectral nature. There was nothing funny about red clay to a funeral man.

George turned and looked at me. "Well, director, what do suppose we ought to do?"

Right then a UPS delivery truck pulled into the church driveway. From the protection of the faded blue tent, we watched the man leap from the truck, dart though the rain, and stop at the back door of the little church. He knocked. And when nobody came to the door, we could see that he was thinking about leaving the brown cardboard parcel there on the back steps, but thought otherwise when he took stock of the rain and what havoc rainwater wreaks on cardboard. Then he spotted us, and at that moment, George had an idea.

The delivery driver was a tall, slender black man with arms the size of Crisco cans. He dashed across the gravel parking lot, leaping over cemetery coping, traversing the standing water like a deity, and finally slid to a graceful stop there in the midst of us; he was, so it seemed to us, sent from above.

"Mornin', men," he said. "I wonder if any of you all happens to be affiliated with this church. I've got a package." He held up the water-stained parcel, the hope and expectation in his eyes more than any of us really wanted to squash.

"Afraid not," said George as he tucked his handkerchief between his t-shirt and right overall strap. "I don't reckon any of us here are in the employ of this here church, but we sure could use your help if you could spare a minute or two."

The delivery man surveyed his surroundings for what I suppose was the first time since he had come upon the property. Six white men, five of whom who were right scruffy looking, all standing around a super-sized casket in the middle of a church cemetery out in the boonies. And to add a little intrigue to the situation, the roughest fellow of all was asking for help.

"Well," the driver said, "exactly what kind of help do you need?"

George smiled, for he knew right then that he had the man. "We're gonna lift this here casket up using these straps. All we want you to do is grab ahold of that handle there on that grave board, and when I tell you to, pull it out. That's all you gotta do."

Right then I saw human suffering at its most primal. That UPS driver was under no obligation to assist us, had no clearly defined duty to us or the dead woman whatsoever. Yet he hesitated. Instead of simply saying "no" and turning on his heels and leaving, he paused. He could have invented an excuse, looked at that rough rope loop that served as the grave board's handle and just walked away. But he stayed; he apparently wasn't used to lying, at least not on such short notice. HE was the kind of man who automatically helped others without forethought or judgment.

George smiled. "Good," he said. "Just grab ahold of that handle and get ready."

I lined up on the backside of the casket with one of the diggers and George. The other three men, basic carbon copies of each other with mud-stained blue jeans, faded t-shirts, and time-wearied grimaces, moved to the front side of the casket. I detected the smell of Wild Turkey from one or all of them. We placed the straps, steadying our footings in the water and mud, and prepared to lift. The delivery truck driver, smiling through his distress, stared at the casket as if he expected the woman inside to leap out at any moment in a fit of divine interference.

I suppose right here would be a good place to explain a bit more about Mrs. Littlejohn's casket. It was what we in the business call a "tall and wide." Its name pretty much says it all. The nondescript casket in battleship gray, the only color we could get on such short notice, was designed, not for beauty or style, but for function. And its function was hold the large Mrs. Littlejohn, to contain her earthly remains. The casket was nothing more than an implement, a conveyance, a tool.

This particular casket came in only one style: half-couch, non-sealer. The term half-couch refers to the fact that the top half of the cap opens, leaving the bottom half closed to cover the waist, legs, and feet. Instead of a rubber gasket to seal the casket and a lock on the foot end, Mrs. Littlejohn's casket came equipped with two dainty metal latches, both on the visible side of the casket, one about even with her elbow, the other even with her lower thigh.

The six of us bent at the knees, put our backs into it, and lifted the tall and wide about foot into the air.

"All right," George instructed the deliveryman. "Pull her out."

The man, his knees a bit shaky and his eyes wide with expectation, withdrew the grave board with a lifer's dexterity. Smooth, easy, flawless. We were impressed.

"Easy does it, boys," purred George. "Let's let her down easy."

At first, everything went just as planned. The head and foot ends of the casket were kept level; we didn't want her sliding to one end and getting all bunched up. There was no bumping or gouging into the red mud sides of the grave. Slow and steady wins the race. But then something happened. The men on the viewing side of the casket, the side visible when a body lays a corpse in the stateroom, began losing their grip. First the head man, then the foot man, then the man in the middle, who found himself bearing all the weight, caved when he could hold no more. In the twinkling of an eye, the casket was on its side. But that wasn't the worst part.

When the casket rolled over onto its side, the straps caught the delicate little latches at the elbow and thigh and popped open the cap. As if that development alone weren't bad enough, because of the position of the now open casket, Mrs. Littlejohn rolled out. Yes, she rolled out of the casket, and all that kept her from tumbling headlong, never to have her girth removed by mere mortal means, into the grave, were those three thin canvas straps that should have been replaced years ago.

The whole chain of events took place in a matter of quick, hasty seconds. In the time it takes to breathe, we found ourselves teetering precariously on the edge of certain litigation.

We continued to lower our side of the casket at a slow, even pace, but the added stress started to wear us down. The straps were pressing into Mrs. Littlejohn's body, groaning against the tension. Thank goodness she was face down and we didn't have to look directly at her.

"Drop this side, men!" George sang out, his voice clear and free of tension. "Let her go."

We released our side of the casket, and it righted itself as the straps sliced through our hands. Mrs. Littlejohn fell back inside, and the casket landed with a marvelous, resounding thump square in the center of the waiting vault.

Somewhere amidst all the confusion, we all heard a high, terrified scream. I suppose what we heard sounded more like a wail than a scream. No one saw the UPS driver drop the grave board or run across the waterlogged parking area. All we saw was a dark brown truck, spinning tires kicking up mud and rock, as it careened out of the narrow gravel parking lot and back down the lonely road from whence it came. We had frightened our savior so that his only recourse was escape. But no matter the outcome, he remained our savior, for without him, nothing would have been possible. Mrs. Littlejohn accepted the grave without objection. Or, perhaps the grave accepted her. Either way, as the waters of a spring rain flowed around us, we went on with our work as if it were any other day.

Ashes to Ashes, Mud to Mud

Getting to Oak Grove Baptist Church from the funeral home usually took about twenty minutes if nothing slowed the regular flow of traffic. Getting to Oak Grove Baptist Church from the funeral home stuck in a funeral procession took nearly forty-five minutes. It was raining on that particular day, so just over an hour after we left the funeral home, we pulled into the puddle-strewn gravel parking lot of the church cemetery. As fate would have it, I was driving the hearse.

The minister, a tall congenial man who had served Oak Grove for over ten years, which by Baptist standards is a lifetime, read his scripture passages, offered the requisite prayer, shook hands with the soggy family members, and said his goodbyes. The family didn't linger either, for their shoes were caked with sticky mud, and the women's hair (and several men's) had flattened beneath thick layers of aerosol-can White Rain hairspray.

My own navy blue suit, wet and sagging, clung to my arms and back. I helped Dave the vault man gather up the plastic chairs and stack them against the metal pole at the back of the second tent. The green carpet grass was too sopping to fold, so we pulled it away from the grave and chucked the pieces near the chairs.

While Dave trudged through the Carolina orange clay to fire up his dolly so he could set the heavy cement cap on the burial vault, its fresh detailing of blue paint already starting to run in the rain, I tiptoed over to the grave to see how the bottom of the vault was faring against the river pouring over the side of the three-foot wide hole. Contrary to public opinion overly swayed by tired Hollywood cliché, the standard human burial grave is not six feet deep; it's more like four feet. In fact, once the average grave is covered, the top of the vault may be only a mere ten-to-twelve inches below the surface.

What I saw when I peered down into the grave surprised me: So much water was running into the grave that the vault had floated up high enough to just about breach the rim of the hole.

"Did you see this?" I asked Larry.

Larry, the sullen grave digger for whom life was little more than one disappointment after another, cleared his throat and spat something brown. "What about it?"

I nudged the side of the protruding vault with the toe of my wingtip. "The vault's about to float out of the grave."

I watched the vault bobbing in the grave, and I was surprised that inside was dry as baby powder. The tent had done its job.

"Ain't nothing a pump won't fix." And he turned toward his white box truck. "Where'd you think all that rain was going anyway, city boy?"

City boy? Nobody had ever called me that before, but I chose to ignore the comment. Judging from the looks of Larry, everybody who wore a suit and tie instead of Dickies coveralls or camouflage Carhartt jackets was probably a city boy to him.

I watched Larry as he strolled back to the tent through the rain and mud. In his gloved hands he held a small portable pump, the kind I've seen at the bottom of swimming pools, and letting the chord slip through his fingers, he dropped the pump between the vault and the side of the grave until it sank to the bottom. With the drain spout pointed down the hill away from the grave, Larry flipped the switch. A generator clanking away inside the dented white truck provided enough power, and after a few seconds of a sputtering hum, orange water began splashing out.

Immediately the vault started to sink back into the grave. I stood out of the way as Larry and Dave worked. When the vault had finally settled as close to the bottom as much as the torrent of rain would permit, the two men released the locks on the chrome-plated lowering device, and the three of us watched in silence as the casket dropped slowly below ground level.

"Go ahead and get the cap on that vault before she starts floating again," Larry said.

Dave guided the slipping and sliding dolly beneath the canvas tent and stopped astraddle the grave. The rattling of the old gas engine and the squeaking of worn out, rusty metal parts provided background music for the lowering of the vault cap. When he'd finished, Dave pulled back on the wet lever and withdrew the cables from the grave. By the time the vault dolly cleared the way, so much rainwater had streamed back into the grave that the vault, this time capped and airtight, floated anew.

I stepped up close and leaned over for a better look inside the grave.

"I wouldn't stand that close to the grave if I was you," Larry grunted.

But before I could ask him why, the waterlogged earth beneath my right foot gave way and I found myself falling into the grave. With my left leg outside the grave and my right leg inside the grave, my foot came to rest on the top of the rocking vault. There I was in a split, and the only thing keeping me from tumbling the rest of the way into the grave was the floating burial vault.

Grinning with pleasure, Larry waited a heartbeat or two before stepping up and offering his hand. "Watch out there, now," he chuckled. "The edge of the grave might cave in with you."

I accepted Larry's hand and sighed as the gravedigger pulled me from the abyss. "Thanks, Larry," I said, my tone unusually curt. "I'll remember that next time."

"Well, see that you do," he laughed. "We can't do our work with you lollygagging around in the grave."

Dave had walked up, and he laughed it up right along with Larry. I looked at my clothes. My pants, soaking with water and orange mud, hung heavy. The bottom half of my coat was covered with mud, too, and my white shirt was ruined. My right shoe went from black to orange in an instant, and I wondered if I would have to discard the pair and start over. Suits, shirts, and shoes cost money, and I hated the idea of throwing any of it away.

I stood off to the side, now right out in the rain, for like a catfish at the bottom of the river, I couldn't get any wetter. Larry and Dave covered the grave without speaking, each shovelful of muddy dirt pushing the vault a little closer to the bottom. After about thirty minutes, an orange, soupy mess covered the grave.

"Ashes to ashes, dust to dust," Dave said, and I wasn't sure, but I thought I detected a hint of sincerity in his voice.

Larry, on the other hand, was not about to be outdone. "And mud to mud," he said, and he shot me a grin.

I rode back to the funeral home that evening in just my boxers and shirt. The suit was ruined, but I did manage to extract the dirt from the shoes and salvage them for another day.

Falling into an open grave was just one of the many hazards of funeral work. Before I would finally leave the funeral business full-time to pursue other pathways, I would give up to the grave the watch my parents had bought me when I graduated from high school, an onyx cuff button, several combs, a pair of Ray Ban Wayfarers, and at least one pack of orange Tic Tacs. But I suppose those temporal items fall short of comparison to all the loved ones claimed by countless graves across the Upstate. As my grandfather was fond of saying: We've all got one foot in the grave and one foot on a banana peel. I suppose he was right on many levels.

Cash or Check?

The hearse driver on a funeral has a litany of responsibilities: park cars for the procession, make sure the casket carriage is in the hearse, roll the casket with the guy on flowers, drive the body out to the cemetery, see that the body is securely in the grave, make sure that any jewelry comes off before lowering the casket into the vault. Seeing to the ultimate whereabouts of all jewelry belonging to the deceased can be a tricky concern, especially when multiple family members with multiple ideas are involved in the multiple steps of the decision-making process.

Like in a lot of families, several members often tend to vie for control, and funerals are no different. On my daddy's side, my Aunt Verna usually takes over: "We're gonna have Christmas at Mama's house this year at exactly six o'clock. Yes, we're having ham again for Easter this year; get over it. Randal's in charge of the fireworks for the 4th of July cookout in Meemaw's back yard. The family reunion this year is gonna be at Hickory Knob State Park. There is no way we're putting mums and baby's breath on Pop's casket."

I hadn't reached my two-year anniversary at the funeral home yet, and I was still driving the hearse. Hoke Harris was the funeral director for the Opal Stone service to be held in our chapel, and he made sure I was out parking cars an hour before funeral time.

"But it's 98 degrees," I protested. "Couldn't I go out a little later? You said we weren't expecting a big crowd."

"Young man," Hoke said, his voice full of old-fashioned Presbyterian preachiness, "you'll be out there at 2:00 o'clock on the dot, and you'll not come in a minute before 2:50. Understood?"

Oh, I understood all right. For the past six months I had
been parking cars before funerals as part of my "training."
Coy Franklin, the funeral director who pretty much ran
the whole show, even though he didn't have the title to go
along with the extra responsibilities, informed me that once
I mastered everything there was to know about driving the
hearse, I could then move on to driving the second family car.
I had worked for over a year learning "everything there was
to know" about driving the flower van, and that job was as
simple as load, unload, and don't destroy; there was no telling
how long I would have to drive the hearse.

After fifty minutes of parking about eight vehicles, and that's
including two preachers' and four pallbearers' cars, I stag-
gered into the basement to wipe my face and guzzle some
cold water.

"Let's get upstairs," Hoke said from around the corner.
"Where've you been? We've got a funeral service to start."

I looked at my watch, let it go, and climbed the stairs.

Once all twenty three family members, both ministers, and
the six pall bearers were behind the closed doors of the
Corner Room for their pre-service prayer, I turned to Hoke
before walking into the state room. "Anything come out of
the casket?"

Confusion was bound to occur for anyone who might over-
hear this question, but Hoke knew that I was referring to the
jewelry or the eyeglasses, perhaps a handkerchief or a family
Bible.

"Everything stays."

I looked down into the casket. Mrs. Stone, who would have
been eighty-six years old on her next birthday, lay all fixed up
and pretty in a dress the family had selected from our exten-

sive collection of burial garments. There was a gold wedding band, a string of pearls, and a thin bracelet. I noticed the dull plastic brooch, which came with the dress and was actually sewn to the fabric, just above a row of five plastic buttons, and I knew no one would want that.

"What about the ring and necklace? Those look real."

Hoke sighed. "The ring is real, but they buried their daddy's wedding band with him, and they want to bury that one with their mama. The pearls are fake. Now close the casket and let's get a move on."

Both preachers preached their hearts out, even though the second one turned out to be a bit longwinded after he realized that he repeated two of the scripture passages used by the first preacher. He even decided, maybe in an attempt to cover up his funeral faux pas, to conclude with an a cappella rendition of the "I'll Meet You in the Morning." I've heard better.

After the committal service, the few people who made the fifty-minute trip to the southern region of the county for the churchyard burial quickly and no-so-discretely exited the cemetery as soon as the second preacher said "Amen." I could tell that Hoke was itching to get back in his lead car, crank up the AC, and head back into town, too. While I flinched at the perspiration rolling down my back and into my Fruit of the Looms, Hoke Harris could stand out in the South Carolina humidity for hours and still not look as if he'd broken a single bead of sweat. And that afternoon was no different. That pallid skin glistened not in the late day sun, nor did the collar of his starched white shirt turn dingy and limp. To this day, I still don't know how he did it.

I watched Hoke take the pouch from the front seat of the Cadillac lead car and walk toward the family. The family member in charge was a daughter, a Mrs. Powell from somewhere near Spartanburg. Hoke smiled, extended his blanched hand, and passed the pouch to Mrs. Powell. I could imagine him saying, "And the pages from the visitation and the service are in there, along with a keepsake book. There are also some acknowledgement cards, two boxes. If you need more, just let me know."

There were muted smiles all around, and just like that, Hoke was gone. The family members tarried a few minutes more, but the swelter of the day finally became too much for them to bear, and they, too, retreated to the comfort of their air conditioned cars. And that left me to a hearse driver's final duties.

Hoke found me the next morning helping Arnie Maddox in the preparation room. We'd gotten three calls during the night, and Arnie, Clyde Combs, and I had been steady going at it since 3:00 AM. Hoke pointed a long index finger at me.

"Young man, step out here with me."

"What'd you do now?" Arnie asked.

I shrugged, peeled off my rubber gloves and smock, washed my hands, and walked through the dressing room toward the basement. I found Hoke leaning against the pickup hearse.

"Where's Mrs. Stone's jewelry?"

I thought for a minute. "Underneath about a foot and a half of red dirt in the Goshen Baptist Church cemetery. Why?"

"You didn't take it off of her?"

"No. You said that nothing came off."

Hoke pondered my reply. In his defense, he had helped two families make their arrangements the day before, worked the Stone service, stayed around the previous night for two visitations, and had already met with another family that morning. I'm sure all that information was jumbled up in his tired brain.

"You sure I said that?"

I smiled. "I am. I asked you right before Clyde and I walked into the room to close the casket."

"Well, that daughter from Spartanburg wants to know where her mama's brooch is." He raised both hands and grabbed the lapels of his coat. "She's waiting in the lobby."

There was a gold ring and a pearl necklace. I remembered those. And that bracelet.

"I don't remember a brooch."

"Come on," he said. "Because they do."

The central air conditioning was already humming along at a steady clip, and the weatherman was calling for another hot one. I had my suit coat on by the time Hoke pushed open the door to the lobby.

Mrs. Powell had her hands on her hips and she was giving her sister an earful, but she purposefully turned her attention to a subdued Hoke. "Well, did you find it?"

Hoke cleared his throat. "This young man here drove the hearse on the service yesterday. He said he doesn't remember seeing a brooch."

"There most certainly was a brooch," the sister said, and she glared at me with scrunched up eyes. "There was Mama's pearl necklace, the bracelet Tina gave her, her wedding band, and the diamond brooch."

"That's right," Hoke agreed. "And Mrs. Powell here said that you all wanted to leave the band, bracelet, and necklace with your mama."

"But that didn't mean you were supposed to leave that brooch on her, too," Mrs. Powell interjected. "I gave her that brooch for Christmas ten years ago."

The sister jerked her head around and puffed up. "Ah, no you didn't. I gave Mama that brooch for her birthday the year before daddy died."

And so it went for a good five minutes, each sister insisting that she was the one who had given her mother the piece of jewelry in question, each one presenting further evidence, evidence, by the way, that grew more absurd with each volley. As the counterpoints flew, the accusations and insinuations grew to the point that the next step after the yelling would be the swinging. Hoke tried unsuccessfully several times to cut them off, but neither one of them was going to let a skinny old undertaker with poufy white hair and a high-pitched Southern accent get in the way.

Finally, after an exasperated Hoke threw up his hands and shook his head in disgust, I offered my say-so. "Excuse me," I said. "Ladies, are you all referring to the brooch pinned on the front of your mother's dress right at the V in the neck-line?"

"Yes," Mrs. Powell snapped. "Of course that's the one we're talking about."

"So you admit that it was on Mama," countered the sister.

Before either woman could continue, I excused myself. When I returned, Hoke, Mrs. Powell, and the sister had resumed their heated discussion.

"I'll sue," threatened the sister.

"No, I'll sue this funeral home," Mrs. Powell told Hoke with a finger wagging just under his long nose, "and I'll sue you, Bertha, if you end up with that brooch. I've had enough of this mess."

"Ladies," I interrupted, "does the brooch in question look like this?"

Mrs. Powell and Bertha leaned forward, their curious eyes glued to the shining piece of jewelry on the front of the dress.

"Yes," said Mrs. Powell. "I'll take it."

"No, it's mine. Give it to me."

I looked to Hoke for some leadership, but he had already stepped back to stifle a wide grin.

"Mrs. Powell. Mrs., umm, Bertha. This is the plastic costume jewelry that comes with the dress." Using my thumb and index finger, I tugged on the diamond brooch. "You see? It's sewn onto this dress. It doesn't come off."

But they didn't see. Early the next morning, Hoke and I met the sisters at Goshen Baptist Church for the disinterment. Their expressions were sour, and they'd brought along with them a variety of stone-faced children and grandchildren to witness "the utter disgrace" of having to "dig up Mama" because "the idiots at the funeral home couldn't remember to take off one tiny, little brooch before they buried her."

Once the grave was opened and the cement vault rested to the side of the hole, Hoke and I moved closer to observe what came next. Because the glue used seal the vault cap to the vault base, well, did its job, the only way to remove the cap from the base was to crack open the vault and cut through the polystyrene lining with a saw. A fresh vault to replace the destroyed one waited in the shade on the back of a flatbed truck.

With the casket exposed, all parties involved jockeyed for position.

"If you all will excuse me, I'll open the casket," Hoke said as the two of us pushed our way through the group.

A few tears emerged, for several people were overcome with newfound grief as Hoke opened the casket.

"Mrs. Powell. Bertha. Would you all step closer, please?"

The sisters huffed and groused a little as they bent at the waist for a closer look.

"Yes, that's it," Mrs. Powell said. "That's very the brooch that I gave Mama."

"No," countered Bertha, "that's the brooch I gave Mama before Daddy died. Give it to me."

Using the thumb and index finger on his right hand, Hoke gave the brooch a tug. "You see, ladies, like the young man told you yesterday when he showed you the dress back at the funeral home, this pin is attached to the dress with thread. It came with the dress. It came with the dress when the dress came to us, the funeral home, from the manufacturer in China."

"I think it was Canada," I added.

Hoke grimaced. "Either way."

Both women straightened up, wiped imaginary grave dirt from their jeans and shirts, and stepped back. Hoke stood, wiped real dirt from the knee of his finely pressed trousers, and waited.

Silence, I've often heard, can be deafening. Deafening, however, is not the word I would use to describe the silence that followed Hoke's concrete, indisputable evidence that strange things were indeed afoot when it came to the daughters' tales concerning the origins of Opal Stone's diamond brooch

"Well," Mrs. Powell finally said. "I guess I was mistaken."

"Yes, it seems that we misunderstood, umm, what we were supposed to do with the jewelry."

Hoke cut his eyes in my direction ever so slightly, and I knew he was about to launch into one of his famous monologues. You see, Hoke had worked in the funeral business for over thirty years. Nothing surprised him. No development caught him off guard. Yes, Hoke Harris had, without a doubt, seen it all.

"Ladies, the misunderstanding came about not only in your refusal to believe us when we told you that the brooch attached to your mother's dress was mere costume jewelry, but also when we actually showed you a similar dress from our collection with the exact pin already attached to the fabric. For whatever reason, you simply refused to take our word for it. While I am in no way here to lecture you, the time has come for us to accept reality."

"You're right," said Mrs. Powell. "We're sorry for the trouble we've caused you."

"Madam, I assure you that this is part of our job and no real trouble to us at all. We're glad to see this issue resolved."

"We are, too," Bertha half-heartedly offered.

"And I'm glad you feel that way," Hoke said as the women turned to leave. "The bill for opening and closing the grave *again* will be $950. The new vault," he pointed toward the idling truck, "to replace the one we ruined will be $1080."

The women's eyes widened and their mouths hung agape. I imagined both of them pondering a $2,030 piece of plastic jewelry. There was nothing they could say.

Hoke smiled. "Will that be cash or check?"

Reflection

FAQs

Now that I spend my days teaching writing and literature instead of driving hearses and flower vans, I find that my students like to ask me "funeral home" questions. When I taught high school, I used this Q&A session as a reward on Fridays for classes who'd met the week's learning objectives. College students, on the other hand, just want to get out of the classroom as quickly as possible, so no such diversions are needed in higher education. Here are a few of the more interesting questions I've been asked through the years:

Question: Do you ever get scared?

Answer: Well, yeah! That first night sleeping in the funeral home was worse than my first Boy Scout winter campout in February when I forgot to pack extra socks. I thought my toes would never warm up the next morning. When I spent my first night in the funeral home so that I could take call, though, it wasn't my toes I was worried about; it was my heart. Every creak of the old building groaning beneath January's frigid winds took another year or two off my life. I convinced myself, against all reason, that something was coming up those creaking stairs from the basement to get me. My wife claims those early years sleeping in the funeral home and waking up at all hours of the night to go on death calls is why I have night terrors now.

As I got used to the idea of working around grief and death and realized that dead means dead, the direction of my fears changed. Instead of fearing the dead, I began to fear the living. No, not everyone who came through the doors frightened me, but I did develop a deep concern that my actions or words might in some small way upset a family during a time of deep distress, the likes of which most of us endure only sporadically in our lives. Do I ever get scared? Yes. Scared that I, through ignorance or haste or self-interest, may make a family's loss of a loved one more painful.

Question: Do dead bodies sit up?

Answer: As my Grandma used to say, "Now, you know better than that." People have told me about funeral directors and morticians who insisted that bodies spontaneously sat up in the middle of embalming, but I've never witnessed it. Don't personally know any embalmers who've seen it, either. The image of torsos jumping up as if on some imaginary spring does make for stimulating conversation, though.

Question: What would you do if a body got up?

Answer: Hmmm. Too many zombie movies, not enough History Channel. No more *Walking Dead* for you!

Question: Do you all take out the guts?

Answer: I believe it's called viscera, and, no, we do not. Think about it. Why would we? If we did, we would just have to put all that stuff some place, and what better place for it than its original container?

Question: Why do y'all cut off the head/legs?

Answer: What kind of television shows are your parents letting you people watch? Nothing gets cut off or taken out.

Well, okay, the blood is taken out, but that's it. All right, hold on. The kidneys, bladder, intestines (both sizes), and lungs are cleared of whatever stuff might be inside them, but the organs stay put. So do heads and extremities.

Question: Do you all rent caskets?

Answer: Believe it or not, yes, we do. How many do you need?

Question: Can I ride in the hearse with you out to the cemetery?

Answer: Front seat or back?

Question: Does working with dead people creep you out?

Answer: Not really. The years have taught me that it's the living ones I need to worry about.

Question: Do you ever regret getting into the funeral business?

Answer: Not at all. After an undergraduate degree and two graduate degrees, I still maintain that I've learned more about life, more about people, working in the funeral home than any college professor could have ever taught me. Why, I've witnessed sights few other professions would ever afford the son of a mill worker-turned-Baptist preacher.

Question: What happens when you cremate a body?

Answer: Fire requires three things: heat, oxygen, and fuel. You probably learned that in 8th grade science. The body is the fuel, sort of. The cremation chamber, jets of fire shooting out from different directions, reaches temperatures of 1400 to 1800 degrees. After a couple of hours, most of the body is consumed by the fire, leaving only the largest bones. After cooling, those bone fragments are then pulverized and placed inside the temporary urn. Sorry you asked?

Question: Are you ever sad?

Answer: I'll admit that most funeral services come and go without my giving them much thought. But there have been those that did affect me. The death of children, for instance, always gets to me. So young, so innocent, so much more to do and see. Yeah, I know it's cliché, but whenever a young person dies, I think about my own children. I remember how fortunate I am to have the time to spend with these children God has so generously blessed my wife and me with, and then I think about how dull and pointless my life would seem without them. That's when the tears threaten. Invariably, my thoughts wander back to the grief-stricken parents forced to bury their young children, and my empathy level surges. Being around so much death on a day-to-day basis is bound to make us sad, and I don't know a single person who's spent any time working in the funeral home who hasn't been touched by the often devastating capriciousness of life.

Ultimately, the sadness that family members experience makes me sad. I'm human. I can't help but relate to the deep sense of loss that accompanies the death of a loved one. I may not have known the deceased or any of their family, and I may be quite used to the same songs and scripture passages that are dusted off at just about every funeral; but that's okay. The loss, grief, and sense of "what now" are new, and as one who will experience that same sadness on a personal level before it's over, I appreciate the pain people must endure.

At the end of the day, I have a new respect for the men and women who work in the funeral business. It can be a difficult life. The emotional toll does catch up with funeral directors, and the fact that they keep coming back even when they've had enough is a testament to the loving, caring natures so many of these men and women possess.

For Sharon, Sadie, and Sloan

About the Author

D.S. Bradley lives in Due West, South Carolina, with his wife and two children. To get through college, he worked as a lifeguard, counted out money as a bank teller, answered the phone at a law firm, sold eye glasses, and sealed and striped parking lots. Since graduating from college, he's taught middle school and high school English, directed a college writing program, and taught college English and writing courses. The experiences, though, that most prepared him for life were the ones he had working as a funeral director. When he's not teaching or writing, he relishes spending time with his family, especially camping, enjoying evening excursions around Due West on the golf cart, or riding his unicycle.

Some of his recent articles and short stories have appeared in *Sandlapper Magazine*, *Family Circle Magazine*, *Fast Company Magazine*, and *State of the Heart: South Carolina Writers on the Places They Love*.

www.ingramcontent.com/pod-product-compliance
Lightning Source LLC
Chambersburg PA
CBHW062309200726

48292CB00004BA/1425